# THE SANCTUARY

OTHER BOOKS BY LARRY RICHARDSON

Desert Heights
The Big Horn*
Showdown at Yellowstone*
The Treasure of Bitter Creek*
The Gold Train*
The Cure for the Common Sermon

*Book descriptions, sample chapters, and
a sample audio chapter available at*
www.lkrichardson.com

*with Tom Richardson

# THE
# SANCTUARY

A NOVEL

## LARRY
## RICHARDSON

DOS HERMANOS

Library of Congress Cataloging-in-Publication Data

Richardson, Larry, author.
The Sanctuary / by Larry Richardson.
ISBN-13: 978-1-7357334-0-1

1. Modern fiction  2. Drama  3. Romance
4. Richardson, Larry

Dos Hermanos Publishing Company
790 Eagle Ridge Drive, Billings MT 59101

❖

ACKNOWLEDGEMENTS

I am grateful to Don Davenport for his essential critiques of narrative, dialogue, and plot development during the preparation of this manuscript. I also wish to thank Officer Daniel Shreeve, with the Billings Police Department, for his assistance in confirming proper police investigation and interview procedures as depicted in this story. Finally, I express my gratitude to my wife Patty for her support, encouragement, patience, critical eye, and keen sense of timing, pace, and story.

❖

# CHAPTER 1

For a few million dollars most anyone will sell their soul, or at the very least, tell you whatever you want to know. And right now a skilled assassin needed the exact whereabouts of two key witnesses preparing to testify in the Giovani crime family trial. Each had enough dirt on Santino Giovani to put him away for life. And with the trial only three days away, these two witnesses hunkered down under the protection of a team of resolute U.S. Marshalls. With their secret location sold to Giovani sympathizers, a paid killer went to work.

In an exclusive Long Island subdivision, the gated homes stood tall as mansions. In this neighborhood any dwelling under 3,000 square feet was considered servants' quarters. The street gutters shined like new, and landscaping made the cover of *Home and Garden* blush. Each compound shimmered in flood lights for dramatic effect.

Halfway down the street an unmarked car parked along the curb. Inside, two U.S. Marshals held vigil.

"How does the universe balance the scales with the scumbag witness we have inside?" one Marshal asked his partner.

"What do you mean?"

"I mean, we're protecting this degenerate so he can testify against his boss, and then walk away scot free."

"Yeah. That's how it works. He who rats first, wins."

"You know, they got another witness ready to testify. That ought to be enough."

"Against the Giovani family? We'll see." The first Marshal picked up his walkie-talkie.

"Streetside to base, come in," he said.

"This is base. What's up?" the voice in the walkie-talkie chirped back.

"You got'em tucked in for the night?" Silence. No reply. "Yo! I said, are they tucked in? Come back." The anxious Marshal from inside the car glanced at his partner.

"I hate it when they screw around like this." Again, he pressed the lever on his walkie-talkie.

"Stop screwing around. Answer back." The two Marshals glanced at each other with mild concern.

"I'm coming in," the Marshal growled into his handset. "Don't shoot me." He checked the loads in his glock and turned to his seatmate.

"You stay on the walkie-talkie. I'm going to have a look-see." He got out of the car and approached the house, service weapon drawn. He slowly opened the front door and entered cautiously. Standing motionless, he scanned the dimly lit room and spotted the Marshal lying on the floor, dead. He approached the body and studied the bullet hole in his head, then moved to the bedroom with heightened caution.

He eased the bedroom door open, gun raised, and peered in. He saw his worst fear realized – the witness and his wife lay in their bed dead, bullets in each head execution style. Just then his walkie-talkie chirped to life.

"How does it look in there? Hello? Come In."

Later that night on Staten Island a two-story warehouse sat quietly in the industrial district. Flood lights illuminated the front wall.

Inside a second-floor room, Leora Wallace sat posing for her husband, Vincent, to paint her portrait. Leora was sixty-three but looked ten years younger. Her flowing brown hair cascaded over her breasts, and her plunging gown presented just the challenge Vincent needed to re-create the look and feel of soft silk fabric conforming to a woman's figure. Vincent, sixty-five, adored his wife of forty years and loved to flatter her with a portrait worthy of Da Vinci. He hoped this little session might distract them from the anxiety of the entire court battle ahead of them.

Vincent stood five feet ten inches tall, with dark black hair sprinkled here and there with tiny streaks of grey. Along his eyes and on his brow a gathering of wrinkles lay. He delicately handled his brush like a surgeon with his scalpel, touching the palette to extract the proper shade of blue, then tapping it lightly on the canvas to create the precise eye color he sought.

"Just turn your head a little to the left," he said, to achieve the perfect glint in her eye. For the last three days the Marshal Service locked these two away for safe keeping until the trial could begin. To while away the down time, Vincent requested a twenty by thirty-inch canvas, easel, a set of brushes, and full palette of acrylic paints. An accountant by profession, he acquired a skill in artistic painting through years of formal training in his spare time. It fed his soul to capture a sunset, a landscape, or a country village on canvas, but he favored portraitures and seemed to have an exceptional eye for the nuances of the human face.

"How much more tonight?" Leora asked.

"Just let me finish your left eye," Vincent said almost in a whisper, to avoid breaking concentration.

From out of the shadows of the parking lot a cell phone beeped. A black hooded guard answered softly.

"Go ahead." The caller's voice registered just below panic level.

"Move the package right now. Get out. Get out now."

"What are you talking about?"

"Our witness is dead, along with an officer. You may be next."

"Where do we go?"

"Just get into the wind. We've already sent back-up. They'll be there any second. Now, GO!" The cell phone caller hung up before the guard could ask any other questions. Without hesitation he burst into the warehouse and called to his partner in a loud whisper.

"Jack! Jack! Where are you? We gotta move." He scanned the room – no Jack. He tiptoed down the hallway, finally spotting Jack walking towards him. "There you are. We gotta get the package out of here." Before Jack could respond, a sniper bullet from a window pierced Jack's neck and he slumped to the floor. The remaining guard dropped to his knees to avoid any exposure to the windows, and crawled to the stairwell to the second floor. Back on all fours he headed for the makeshift bedroom. Rolling over on his back, he kicked Vincent's door open.

"Vincent! Leora! Get up! We gotta go!" From their makeshift studio, the remaining witness and his wife stood upright.

"What the hell?" said Vincent.

"What's happening?" Leora asked.

"We've been hit. Jack's dead. I gotta get you out of here. Drop your things. Let's go!"

From the shadows the assassin entered the building. No sooner did he get inside, cars squealed into the parking lot, and back-up Marshals poured out. The assassin downed the nearest Marshal with his glock, to hold the rest at bay, then headed up the staircase. The commanding officer grabbed his handset to warn the warehouse guard inside.

"He's in the building. Get out. Get out." The guard inside could not be sure of the safest way out, so he pushed Vincent and his wife into a corner of their room where a temporary bed sat pushed against the wall. In his haste, Vincent accidentally kicked the easel and knocked over the canvas, which fell in their direction. The guard sat them on the floor and threw a mattress over them. Then he flipped a desk on its side and hunkered down, praying for reinforcements.

The assassin quickly stepped over the victim of his sniper bullet, up the stairs, and down the hallway, in search of his intended target. Marshals raced to the rescue, climbing the stairs and spotting the assassin.

"Drop it. Drop your weapon. You are surrounded," the forward Marshal called out. The assassin dropped to his knee and began firing at the forward Marshal. From the other end of the hallway more Marshals converged. The assassin turned on his heels and fired at the new threat. Time was running out. He broke through the door to Vincent's room, where the warehouse guard sat waiting. The guard fired, but missed – his last mistake. The assassin returned fire and killed the guard with a single shot. His body fell backward against the mattress.

As his body dropped to the floor, the mattress flopped over, exposing Vincent and Leora. The assassin saw his last chance to finish the job. Both Vincent and Leora knew they were about to die. As the assassin took aim, Leora threw her body over Vincent, taking the first shots. Her blood splattered the floor and scattered drops on the unfinished canvas, adding her blood red to the portrait dress. The assassin changed clips to finish off the star witness, when Marshals burst into the small room. In the exchange of close-quarter gunfire one Marshal was hit, but the assassin was shot and killed. Other Marshals ran to Vincent.

"Are you all right?" one Marshal asked. Vincent could not answer. He turned to see the lifeless body of his loving wife, who sacrificed her life to save his. He scooped her up in his arms and wept.

# CHAPTER 2

The courtroom burst to overflowing. Vincent Wallace sat resolute in the witness stand, his eyes fixed on Santino Giovani at the defense table. The prosecuting attorney fired the crucial question at Vincent.

"Mr. Wallace, do you see the man responsible for ordering the killings of those twelve rival gang members and the bombing of Alamande Hall in Queens?" Vincent looked Santino Giovani straight in the eye.

"Yes, I do."

"Would you point him out to the jury and the courtroom?" Vincent and Santino Giovani locked eyes on each other. Vincent raised his arm and pointed to Santino.

"He is right there." The courtroom exploded in reactions to this damning testimony. The gaze between Santino and Vincent remained fixed as Santino slowly pointed right back at Vincent.

"Let the record reflect that Mr. Wallace pointed to Santino Giovani," the attorney said. Vincent continued.

"That's right, I'm pointing at you, you god-damned murderer. You don't scare me. I'm already dead. You killed my wife, so I don't care what happens to me." The judge rapped the gavel.

"Order in the court! And Mr. Anderson, will you please restrain your witness." Vincent stood up in the witness stand.

"I hope you burn!" he said. The courtroom bedlam escalated.

Santino Giovani stood up to assert himself with this dead man on the stand. His attorney tried to restrain him.

"Mr. Giovani, please sit down. This is not over."

"That's right you scumbag," Vincent said. "Sit your ass back down."

The prosecuting attorney approached Vincent. "Mr. Wallace, please step down off the stand and shut your mouth," he said. Vincent stood up, considering the possibility lunging for Santino's throat. But two of Santino's sons surrounded their father in case things got out of hand. The courtroom descended into a free-for-all. The judge again pounded his gavel.

"Bailiff – clear the courtroom! We are in recess until further notice." Court officers surrounded Santino Giovani and began escorting him out, but he refused to take his eyes off Vincent. Other officers locked arms around Vincent and began leading him out a separate door. Vincent strained to return the stare-down. Santino gave him a smile and a nod as his final farewell.

Vincent, in the clutch of U.S. Marshals, walked briskly down the hallway and through an open door into an office. Once inside, the door closed behind them. The lettering on the door's glass window read "U.S. Federal Witness Protection Service."

The U.S. Penitentiary in Marion, Illinois, became Santino's new home. In the prison's visiting room, Johnny Giovani, Santino's son, sat at a table as a prison guard escorted Santino Giovani in his prison jumpsuit. Johnny sat across from his aging father. In his mid-thirties, Johnny cut a lean figure, wiry, not muscular. He looked image-conscious, clean shaven with brown hair that looked too well manicured to imagine he did it himself. His wardrobe showed impeccable taste, no doubt the guidance of a trusted tailor.

"You're lookin' good, Pops. They feedin' you OK?"

"You travel all the way from New York to talk about food?"

"Pops!"

"For the last three years I been reading the paper every day just for the obits. Every day I read the obits and I'm lookin' for one name. For three years I'm lookin' for just one name!"

"Pop, we're lookin' everywhere. I got eyes on his kids, his friends, his old school mates, everyone he ever worked with. I'm turnin' over every stone. Whata ya want?"

"I'm serving two life sentences and he's still breathing air. I want him dead."

"I do too. I'm tryin' hard."

"Listen, Johnny, I'm done. This is your business now. Everyone is looking at you. What are you gonna do? You let this guy skate and you're out of business."

"I hear you."

"You need somebody who does this for a living. Someone who specializes in this sort of thing."

"Like who?"

"One of the guys in here, he's here 'cause he got tagged by this guy who knows how to find people, you know, people who don't wanna be found."

"Yeah – OK."

"This guy's an expert in this thing called 'skip tracing'. I recommend you get that guy and you turn him loose."

"Just give me his name." Santino slipped him a folded piece of paper with contact information.

"They call him Mr. Diamond."

In the New York City garment district a clean multi-storied warehouse sat along a row of similar structures lined with delivery trucks. Johnny's office perched on the top floor. Spacious and stylish, it showcased fine artwork and tasteful furnishing. Johnny sat at his desk reviewing ledgers, when he heard a knock at the door.

"Come in." The door opened from the outside by a suited heavy, and Mr. Diamond entered, wearing a dark grey Armani suit, well cut, and striking. His touch of grey hair put him in his sixties. His gait, posture, and poise told Johnny he had the right man. Johnny stood up to shake hands.

"I'm Johnny Giovani."

"Mr. Diamond."

"Please sit down. Can I offer you something?" Mr. Diamond politely waved him off and shook his head. Johnny returned to his desk.

"Mr. Diamond, you came highly recommended. You may know my father, Santino Giovani."

"I've heard of him."

"I understand you specialize in skip tracing."

"I find people."

"If you don't mind my asking, how did you come by this line of work?

"I used to work with the Bureau chasing down bad guys – ten most wanted, that sort of residue. Found I had a knack for it. Now I'm strictly private."

"So, you're like a bounty hunter?"

"Not quite. I just find them. I don't bring them in."

"Oh, OK. Well, we've been looking for a certain guy for three years with no luck."

"Mr. Giovani, this has become a very small world. They found Bin Laden in the third floor of a Pakistan compound. Trust me, with the technology today, nobody can hide for long anymore." Johnny slid a heavy file on the desk over to Mr. Diamond to peruse.

"The gentleman I'm looking for is highly motivated to remain invisible. He may not even be in this country anymore, and he's probably changed his looks." Mr. Diamond flipped through the pages of the file.

"Doesn't matter. Even with the rinky-dink facial recognition software they use in Vegas, you could pick him out in a crowd in a heartbeat."

"I like what I hear so far."

"What's your interest in this individual?"

"He used to work for us. Let's just say he left without his sever-ance package. That file will tell you everything about him – family, friends, jobs, places he's lived." Mr. Diamond scanned the file. He stopped at a page listing "hobbies".

"I see he has one hobby listed – painting."

"Yeah – so?" Mr. Diamond rose to leave.

"I'll be in touch."

"So, you'll find him?" Mr. Diamond stopped and turned.

"Our success rate is ninety-four percent. If we find him, I'm going to hand you a piece of paper with his address on it. What you do with that address is your business. But you're going to write me a check for two million dollars when I do. Agreed?" Johnny had to think about that for a moment.

"Suppose he's not at that address when we get there?"

"I don't cash the check until you consummate your reunion. Are we agreed?"

"OK – agreed." They shook hands.

"In my line of work a handshake is binding. When I cash the check, if it's declined, I will call on you one more time. That is a visit you don't want. And believe me, if I can find him, I can for damn sure find you, whether you're holed up here or hiding in a cave in Afghanistan. Are we clear?"

"We're clear. How long does it usually take?"

"Two days was the fastest. Eight months was the longest – that was an African monarch hiding in exile. Trust me – they all get found."

# CHAPTER 3

The Terracina Grand Retirement Community enjoyed year-round sun and mild winters, typical of Orlando, Florida. Built to offer seniors a high level of elegance and luxury, the campus featured 350 apartments, 100 villas, extensive landscaping, and a beautifully appointed clubhouse framed with palm trees. The community stood as the flagship of the United Senior Living Corporation, headquartered in Chicago, Illinois. On this day, a celebration drew hundreds of guests to the clubhouse for hors d'oeuvres, champagne, and congratulations. A live band played standards as waiters slipped through the room with champagne flutes on platters.

A few key executives converged around the refreshment table. Darryl Brooks, the company's Director of Operations, held court with a cluster of fawning VPs and regional directors. Darryl was fifty-five years of age, stout, with thinning hair and a mixture of charisma and drive. His underlings saw this night as an essential opportunity to point out their individual achievements to Darryl in hopes of securing notice and advancement. However, the night belonged to Phil Branson, the executive director of Terracina Grand, celebrated by senior management for filling this community in record time.

Phil was forty, sharp, successful, capable. He stood a shade under five feet eleven inches, with a build that flattered any suit –

broad in the shoulder, narrow at the hip. He could have lettered in football, but found colliding with 280-pound linebackers un-appealing. He wasn't a dandy – he could get dirty when the job required it. In fact, he looked downright sexy in a sweaty T-shirt and knockabout jeans. His natural good looks and winning smile disarmed friend and foe alike.

As a youth growing up in Florida, he loved the beach and knew he must one day own a house on the water. He attended college at the University of Central Florida, majoring in business adminis-tration, just because he did not know what he wanted to do with his life, and decided business administration would open a lot of doors, if ever he could figure out which one to walk through.

He occasionally joined his mom when she visited her parents, who lived in a large retirement community in Orlando called The Mayflower. It was quite elegant, and his grandparents seemed safe and content. His mother introduced him to Bob Summers, the ex-ecutive director, a man who seemed to possess the easiest job in the world, in Phil's estimation. After all, how much work does it take to feed and entertain a couple hundred grandmas, he thought. Occasionally, he caught the executive director in action, acting like a man running for office, smiling, glad-handing, schmoozing with the residents, always ready with a joke and a laugh. Phil gave him props for a good memory. He remembered everybody's name – even Phil's.

On the eve of his graduation from UCF, Phil got a phone call from Summers.

"Phil, we're starting an assistant administrator program here, and I wondered if you might be interested. With your BA this could be a terrific springboard for you." Phil had no immediate summer plans, other than beach volleyball.

"How much does it pay?" Phil asked.

"You'd get a stipend, but mostly you'd get experience – on-the-job training under my wing."

"Why me?"

"I got a feeling about you. Your mom told me some good things, and I think you're going places. Why not here?"

One thing Phil always liked about his dad – if he couldn't think of a reason to say no to something, he'd agree with a jovial "I don't see why not." And right now seemed the perfect moment to invoke his father's rule of life. He signed on, thinking it would just be for a few months. Three years later, Phil practically ran the place. Under Bob Summers' deft leadership, he learned to read a profit-loss statement, oversaw staffing plans, figured out the secrets of running a high-class dining room on a budget, hired and oriented new employees, and worked hand-in-hand with the state to deliver three straight deficiency-free surveys.

"I owe you an apology," he confessed to Summers one evening after work. "When I first signed on, I thought your job was easy. Now I know it is anything but that – you just made it look easy."

"Yeah, sometimes I feel like the duck on a pond – above water he's gliding along smooth as silk, but under the water where nobody can see, he's paddling like crazy."

In 2005 the parent corporation, at the recommendation of Summers, offered Phil the plum position as the executive director of The Devonshire Club, a sprawling senior community in West Palm Beach. While there he met his future bride, Sherry Hadley. Sherry worked as a visiting physical therapist, and the two clicked immediately, like two pieces of a puzzle that fit together perfectly. They made each other laugh, loved the same kind of movies, music, and restaurants. They married one year after they met, and Phil knew his life was now complete.

Phil never believed the old Greek adage that before the gods tear you down, first they build you up. But six months after the happy couple returned from their honeymoon, Sherry was killed in a car accident on her way to work, leaving Phil a hopeless emotional wreck. For the next year he pinballed between pain, anger, depression, and despair. The world lost its color, and every day appeared a dark grey haze. Through the love and patience of family and co-workers he managed to get control of his emotional wheel and level out. Friends gently urged him to start dating again, but he declined their well-intended advice. He knew there could never be another Sherry. And he would not settle for less.

For the next twelve years Phil poured himself into his work and made the Devonshire Club the most envied senior community in South Florida. Under his guiding hand, the waiting list to move in grew to two years. The Devonshire Club made the cover of *Retirement Today*, *Where to Retire*, and *Florida Living Magazine*.

In 2017 United Senior Living Corporation recruited Phil to oversee the opening and fill-up of the Terracina Grand in Orlando. He achieved that goal in record time, and tonight the company saw fit to praise him for this stellar achievement.

"This is your night, Phil. Soak it up," said Darryl. Phil tipped his champagne flute.

"Thanks."

"No. Thank YOU. You took this retirement center from start-up to fill-up in record time. Very impressive."

"I had some help." Darryl coaxed Phil into a quiet corner to talk about the future.

"I appreciate your modesty, but success doesn't happen by accident. The company owes you, Phil. We're talking promotion, and a new location."

"I'm listening."

"You know we've got that big retirement campus under construction down in Palm Beach."

"Yeah – Wellington Estates."

"It'll be our new flagship. It's going to make Del Webb and Sun City weep."

"I'll send Kleenex." Darryl paused for a moment and cleared his throat.

"Here's the thing. It's not going to be ready for another twelve months. They're still pouring concrete."

"I can wait. I'm doing fine here in Orlando."

"You may be doing fine, but we're not."

"What do you mean?"

"We've got a retirement center out west that's really sucking wind right now. The administrator just left and we haven't found a replacement yet."

"So?"

"We need a troubleshooter. A fixer. Someone who can get it back on its feet and put it on the map. Someone like you. That's what you do best."

"Where exactly is this problem child?" Phil said.

"Billings," Darryl said. Phil cringed slightly.

"Billings – as in Montana?"

"It's called The Sanctuary. It's a nice place. Two hundred twenty apartments."

"People actually retire to Montana?"

"Now, wait. Before you say no, just hear me out. We've got a lot invested in that facility. Independent living, assisted living, and memory care. And the chairman has a soft spot for it. But it's hemorrhaging money."

"I don't know. I'm not really a wild west kind of guy. I'm kind of partial to the coast. What's the problem out there?"

"They've got that place twisted up in twenty different ways. It'd take a week just to explain it all."

"And I'm supposed to fix it?"

"You've got the Terracina Grand here on auto-pilot now. You're going to be bored here. You need a new challenge."

"How long we talking?"

"Just till we find a permanent guy. Six, eight months tops. Then you're on your way to Palm Beach, sun and sand – all the way to Easy Street."

"And what if it's not fixed in eight months? You gonna pull Palm Beach out from under me?"

"That's going to be your incentive to get it done."

"You're going to have to do better than that. You need to make it worth my while."

"Like what?"

"For starters, a bonus for cash flowing the project ahead of schedule."

"What kind of bonus?"

"Oh, let's say twenty-five percent of whatever I save you in negative cash flow."

"That could be a quarter million."

"But look how much you'll be making."

"You want my shirt too?"

"Let me think about it. I've never even seen the place. Talk about buying a pig in a poke."

"Fair enough. I've got a whole file on The Sanctuary in my car. Take it home and read it."

Phil spent the night weighing his options. He was always a team player and never shrank from a challenge. He pored through the information packet Darryl gave him. The financial statements looked frightful. Staffing was all wrong, and debt service seemed out of whack. In the morning he called Darryl.

"All right. I'll give it ten months. Then I'm moving to Palm Beach, ready or not."

"Deal."

# CHAPTER 4

In late April, Phil peered out the window of his commuter plane as it banked north for final approach. Beneath him lay Billings, Montana, a modest community along the Yellowstone River, surrounded by an immense untamed wilderness. Despite its unassuming footprint, Billings ranked as the largest city in the state, with over three times the population of Helena, the state capital. The plane taxied to the gate as the flight attendant welcomed everyone to Montana.

"You're kidding," he thought, as he disembarked. He counted eight gates along the concourse – eight. "Orlando must have eighty gates," he thought. He did appreciate the short walk to baggage claim – no trams, shuttles, or human conveyor belts. He collected his bag and headed for the exit door and the taxi stand. A lady holding a sign reading "Welcome Phil Branson" stood next to the information booth.

"I'm Phil Branson."

"I'm Annie Belmont."

"Are you the welcoming committee?"

"Yeah. I'm the office manager for The Sanctuary. I'm here to pick you up." She looked to be in her late-thirties, trim figure, sharply dressed, with a smile like you'd been away too long. She didn't quite have Bette Davis eyes, but they were striking anyway. Her sandy brown hair extended to just above her shoulders, pulled back behind her ears to offer full view to her modest earrings.

"Well, thank you. I was just getting ready to hail a taxi." Annie looked him over.

"First things first – do you own a cowboy hat?" she asked.

"No."

"Boots?"

"No."

"Then, we're going shopping," she smiled.

"We are?" Phil said. "This won't pass inspection?"

"Not in this town. I'm not going to let you embarrass yourself on your first day." She walked him to the Chevy Suburban in the parking lot.

"This is a company car – it will be yours as long as you're here," Annie said. They loaded his luggage and drove into town.

"We've got a manager's apartment on the third floor ready for you. End of the hallway. Two bed, two bath. Balcony. Nice view."

"Sounds perfect."

They pulled into Lou Taubert Ranch Outfitters, a Billings tradition for western wear since 1919. When they walked in the door, Annie gave Luke, the store manager, a wave.

"How ya doin', Annie?" Luke called out.

"Got a customer for ya," she said, pointing to Phil. "You need to set him up, top to bottom – hat, shirt, Wranglers, belt, and boots. Gotta make him look like a local."

"We can do that." He turned to Phil. "What's your budget?" Phil shrugged his shoulders.

"Whatever it takes."

"OK – let's get to it."

An hour and $1,250 later, Phil looked like a native Montanan. He wore a Stetson like Gus McCrae in "Lonesome Dove." They even aged it a bit to give it that worn look, not stiff and shiny like a city slicker. He rocked a cobalt blue western shirt, Wranglers, Lucchese boots, and a corduroy blazer coat. He checked himself out in the three-way mirror.

"Now you're talkin'," Annie said. "You look dangerous – and I mean that in a good way," she said with a wink. They got back in the Suburban.

"Where you from?" Annie asked.

"Orlando," Phil said.

"Florida?"

"Yep."

"I've never been there," Annie confessed.

"That's OK. We're even, 'cause I've never been to Billings."

"You here for the duration, or are you just the fix-it man?"

"Why do you ask?" Phil said.

"Well, you came alone, like you don't plan on staying."

"I'm not married."

"Well, if you let it, this place will grow on you."

"Are you from here?" Phil said.

"Born and raised."

"You ever been out of Montana?"

"I lived in LA for three years."

"Really?"

"Yeah – I was gonna be an actress. Waitressing by night, casting calls by day."

"How'd it go?"

"I got my name out there. Things looked like they were starting to break my way, bit parts, you know. Directors were getting to know me, and sooner or later there's going to be that special role and they're gonna think of me. That's how it works."

"But you're here now?" Phil said.

"Yep. LA didn't work out. Anyway, back to business – the day shift is waiting for us. They were hoping we could have a short little meet 'n greet," Annie said. "Is that OK with you?"

"For sure. I'd like that," Phil said.

They pulled into the parking lot of The Sanctuary, an impressive three-story retirement community with a large porte cochere, extensive landscaping, and heavily wooded forest buffering the community from the open range to the rear. Phil approved.

"This looks nice," he said. Why would a place like this be in trouble? he thought. They parked in the administrator's reserved parking space, the nearest slot to the front door. He shook his head as he got out of the car.

The gathering met in the central dining room in the afternoon. Everyone was in uniform, looking their best – kitchen, housekeeping, office, maintenance, activities, personal care, and marketing – about forty in all. Phil stepped to the front.

"I want to say thank-you to everybody for the nice welcome. And I'll tell you, I like what I see here. You all look sharp. I'm going to get to know each of you when I visit your departments. This facility is called 'The Sanctuary' – that's a perfect name, a safe haven for its residents and a secure place to call home. And together we're going to get it pointed in the right direction." The staff gave Phil a polite round of applause. He put on his Stetson and modeled it. "How do I look?" Everyone chuckled. In self-mockery he imitated a bow-legged cowboy. The staff laughed and gave him another round of applause.

Phil decided the first order of business was to meet the outgoing administrator, Walter Angler. If anyone knew what the facility needed, he felt Walter should. He drove out to Walter's home just before dinner. The residence was a stylish ranch-style home in one of the nicer subdivisions in Billings. Phil rang the doorbell. The door opened and Walter appeared. He was lean, with thinning hair and age lines along his eyes and brow, which was certainly understandable, since he was in his late sixties. He looked tired.

"So, you're my replacement," Walter said cordially. "Come on in." They got comfortable in the living room. Clara Angler, his wife, joined them to ask for drink orders.

"Can I offer you anything to drink? Water? Tea? Vodka?" she offered. Phil smiled.

"We'll see how the conversation goes. I might need a vodka, depending on what Walter has to say."

"Thanks, dear. I think we're OK for now," Walter said. His wife excused herself.

"So, this is what retirement looks like," Phil said.

"I'm rather flattered that it took someone like you to fill my shoes. I've been reading about you in the company newsletter. You're quite the golden boy right now."

"Yeah. Well, this too shall pass."

"You got that right. I was the golden boy once. I saw you at a company convention a few years ago when you were up and coming. I said to myself 'He's going to have your job one day.' Now just look, here you are."

"Why'd you retire, Walter?"

"I think everybody should know when it's time to go."

"I don't mean to talk out of school, but the home office thinks you tied this place into a knot then ran off."

"There's a lot of stuff going on here that they don't know about. And maybe some stuff even you don't need to know."

"Like what?" Phil asked.

"It's stuff you can't fix."

"Maybe. Maybe not."

"For starters, why don't you take a look at the financial statements and compare the debt service from 2018 to 2019. That's all I'm going to say."

"Why? What am I going to find?"

"Just do it. And welcome to The Sanctuary."

First thing the next morning Phil stepped out on the balcony of his manager's apartment and smelled the crisp Montana air. He looked out at the woods just beyond the back patio and saw deer quietly grazing.

"That's something you don't see in Orlando."

He stepped off the elevator on the first floor and walked to his office. Annie was already at her desk.

"Morning, Mr. Branson," she said. He smiled.

"You're here bright and early," he replied. "And just call me Phil."

"OK, Phil."

"Could you bring me the financial statements for 2018 and 2019?"

"Sure." Before he could pour himself a cup of coffee from the work room, she laid them on his desk. He rolled up his sleeves and pored through them, picked up the phone and dialed Annie.

"Annie, get me the ownership file for this facility. Thanks." He continued to sift through the financial statements, making a series of notes. Annie entered with a notebook and set it on his desk.

"Here it is."

"Thanks. Oh, and a couple more things." He pulled out a small note pad from his pocket. "I need a list of all the apartments and highlight the ones that are vacant."

"OK."

"Next, I need a list of everyone who is delinquent on their rents."

"You got it."

"Then tell the maintenance director," he paused to check the employee roster, "Hank Reilly, tell him I'd like to see him." Annie jotted that down.

"And one last thing. Take the administrator's name plate off the reserved parking space out front. Have a new plate made."

"What do you want it to say?"

"Employee of the week," Phil said. Annie smiled.

"OK." She excused herself as Phil studied the chain of ownership for The Sanctuary. He picked up the phone and dialed the home office in Chicago.

"United Senior Living," said the receptionist.

"Hi, this is Phil Branson. Is Darryl Brooks in?"

"Oh, hi, Phil. Yeah, I'll transfer you." Phil held for a moment.

"This is Darryl."

"Darryl, this is Phil out in Billings."

"Well, howdy, partner. How's the weather out there where the west commences?"

"Why didn't you tell me you were a part owner in this place?"

"Well, you have been a busy bee, haven't you."

"No, you're the one who's been busy. You sold this place from one limited partnership to another in 2019 and pocketed a million dollars, then dumped the extra debt service on the project."

"That's really none of your concern."

"Oh, I think it is. That little stunt added another ten grand to the monthly mortgage payment, which means this place won't cash flow till it hits ninety percent."

"Just raise the rents, Phil. You know how it works."

"We can't raise rents when we're seventy percent occupied."

"Well, that's your choice. You can cut salaries if you want. I don't care. Just remember, your bonus doesn't kick in till you cash flow."

"So, it's like that? OK, well played."

# CHAPTER 5

As soon as Phil got off the phone, Annie popped her head in the door.

"Mr. Branson, I mean, Phil – Hank's here."

"Thanks, Annie." Phil left his office and passed through the work room to greet Hank Reilly, the maintenance director. Hank was in his fifties, fit and trim for a man his age, with a life of experience at fixing everything from toasters to diesel generators. He wore his starched green utility shirt with his name stitched onto the breast pocket. Phil noticed. He shows pride in his appearance and his profession, Phil thought. I like that.

"You hollered?" Hank said.

"Yeah. You're the maintenance director?"

"Yep. Hank Reilly." They shook hands.

"Well Hank, let's go for a walk."

"Why not." Annie handed Phil a clipboard.

"All the apartments. The empties are highlighted in yellow," she said. Phil gave her a wink.

"Thanks."

Phil and Hank turned in the direction of the first-floor apartment corridor. They passed by the piano lounge where several residents, mostly female, gathered for a sing-along. Lester, the activity director, sat at the baby grand piano, playing old familiar tunes, slow and sad. Phil took notice as they walked by.

"How long you been here, Hank?"

"Since opening day – 'bout ten years." Phil scanned the ceiling tiles.

"How's she holding up?"

"She's in good shape."

As they walked down the hallway, Mrs. Walsh approached, fashionably dressed and sporting well-coiffed silver hair. Hank gave Phil a quick heads-up.

"Here comes Mrs. Walsh. Plenty of money and a lot of opinions." Phil nodded his head. He knew the type.

"Are you the new manager?" she asked.

"Yes, Phil Branson. And you're Mildred Walsh?"

"Well, yes I am. How did you know?" Phil ignored the question.

"What a treat. And how are you liking The Sanctuary?"

"I just hope you can do a better job than our last manager."

"What's the problem?"

"Mr. Branson, you have to do something about the food. I pay a lot of money to live here, and it's just not acceptable."

"Anything in particular?"

"The veal is dry, the lettuce is wilted, and the vegetables are always over-cooked."

"You're right – I'd be upset too."

"And only four shrimp in my shrimp cocktail. Everyone knows it should be five or six – not four."

"I'll speak to the chef." Mrs. Walsh looked him up and down.

"We'll see. I know people. I don't have to put up with this." She turned to Hank. "And Mr. Reilly, now that I think of it, the hot water in my apartment is never hot enough."

"I'll check it out." Mrs. Walsh wagged her finger for emphasis.

"I don't have to live here, you know. Other retirement communities in this town would love to have me." She turned and continued down the hallway. Hank leaned in to Phil.

"You wanna bet?" he whispered.

"Now, that is one squeaky wheel that needs some grease," Phil said. They continued their walk. Phil made a note on the clipboard.

"What exactly are we doing?" Hank said.

"Checking something out." They stopped in front of apartment 183. Phil looked at his clipboard, then knocked. They heard a voice coming from inside.

"Yes?" Phil looked at the clipboard again.

"This is supposed to be vacant," he said. The door opened and one of the housekeepers appeared.

"Can I help you?"

"I don't think we've met," Phil said.

"This is Louisa Martin. She's one of the laundry workers," Hank said.

"Are you cleaning this unit?" Phil said.

"No, I live here."

"Uh, OK." The housekeeper closed the door. Phil turned to Hank for an explanation.

"Two sisters work in the laundry department, and the last administrator let them live here for free instead of paying them a salary."

"How long's that been going on?"

"Four years." Phil shook his head and made another note on the clipboard.

"Darryl, Darryl, Darryl," Phil muttered. They turned and retraced their steps to the office and passed by the piano lounge, where the sing-along continued. The ladies sat around the edge of a small dance floor, along with one gentleman, listening politely. But no one chose to dance. Phil noticed the dreary mood. He handed his clipboard to Hank.

"Hang on a sec." Phil walked over to the dance floor and approached Mrs. Cohen. She was in her seventies, dressed fashionably, with an attractive silver hairdo. Phil extended his hand to her.

"Would you do me the honor?" Mrs. Cohen blushed at the invitation, but accepted. Phil took her by the hand to the middle of the dance floor and turned to Lester at the piano.

"Lester, give me a samba." Lester began playing a classic samba tune as Phil and Mrs. Cohen treated the crowd to a smooth and easy samba. The lone gentleman invited one of the ladies to dance, and soon others joined in and the dance floor came alive with residents dancing. One determined widow cut in on Mrs. Cohen to have her turn dancing with Phil. At the end of the tune Phil gave his dance partner a gentle dip, then lifted her back up as the crowd broke into applause. Phil walked over to the lone gentleman to introduce himself.

"Thanks for joining in," Phil said, as he extended his hand. "My name's Phil Branson. I'm the new executive director."

"Dexter Bailey," the gentleman answered back. "Pleased to meet you."

Phil sized him up quickly – a dandy, for sure. A full head of silver-white hair professionally manicured. Dressed to the nines with a monogrammed handkerchief in his coat pocket. Dexter was a dapper widower in his early seventies, with a lean and graceful body that nature had been kind to.

Phil and Hank excused themselves and continued to the main office.

"What do you know about Dexter?" Phil asked.

"He's single, and quite the lady's man," Hank said.

"Good for him – this is a target-rich environment, that's for sure," Phil said.

Before they got to the office, Susan Phillips, the marketing director, intercepted them. She was a no-nonsense woman in her fifties, professionally dressed, with that go-give aura about her.

"Mr. Branson, could I have a word?"

"Susan, anytime the marketing director wants to talk, I'm all ears."

"OK. Here's the thing, I've got a couple from Miles City who want a two-bedroom on the first floor close to the dining room."

"Move 'em in."

"The only one like that is being occupied by two laundry workers."

"Oh, yeah, I just met them."

"I was told by the last administrator not to rent that apartment to anyone. So I just want to know what's your policy." Phil gave Hank a look, then turned to Susan.

"Rent it." Susan broke into a smile.

"I will." Phil and Hank returned to the office.

"This should be fun," Hank said.

That afternoon the facility conference room filled with the department heads – marketing, housekeeping, maintenance, food service, activities, and personal care. Cookies and coffee sat ready for all takers. Each department gave a brief report on their activities and goals. Phil stood at the whiteboard with marker pen in hand making notes. The clock on the wall read 4:15.

"All right, the last department we're going to hear from is marketing. Susan?" Susan stepped to the whiteboard.

"Thanks, Mr. Branson. I am happy to report that we just rented the two-bedroom on the first floor – the one the laundry workers have been living in." The room offered her a round of applause. "Yeah, I know. That puts us at seventy-two percent and climbing. I've got four reservations for move-ins later this month, so Hank, I'm going to need to get with you after this meeting be make sure they're ready to go. That's it for now." She returned to her seat. Phil stood up.

"OK. One last item. You've probably noticed that the administrator's reserved parking space has been changed to the 'employee of the week.' That means that everybody gets to use that space one week out of the year. Annie will print up a sheet so you can see which week is yours." Fran, the housekeeping director, raised her hand. She was in her fifties, neat and trim in her uniform.

"Yes, Fran?" Phil said.

"That include all my housekeepers?"

"Everyone."

"What do you have to do to win?"

"Nothing. Just work here."

"Where are you gonna park?" Hank asked.

"I don't know. As far away as possible. I need the exercise." He slapped his flat belly and the staff chuckled. "OK, everyone, this place is looking sharp and you're all doing fantastic. Let's go get'em."

# CHAPTER 6

The central dining room at The Sanctuary was located on the first floor, just off the lobby. It was a large hall with a seating capacity for over 200, and it made quite an impression on first-time visitors. White tablecloths and cloth napkins gave the room an elegant touch, and the small bouquet of flowers at each table added color and charm. Lunchtime enjoyed the largest turnout of residents. It was the main meal of the day and an important social event. On this day the wait staff brought plates of spaghetti to each table, just like a regular restaurant. Resident chatter reminded everyone of the importance of human interaction at any age. Lester warmed up the room with live piano tunes, creating an inviting atmosphere.

Phil and Annie stood at the perimeter of the dining room. Phil studied the speed and quality of service, and noted the expressions on the residents' faces. He noticed Dexter Bailey wearing a stylish ascot and holding court with a table full of silver-haired ladies, all dolled up and vying for attention. As Phil scanned the other tables, he noticed Mrs. Walsh, his food critic, was missing.

"Where's Mrs. Walsh?"

"The griper? I don't know." Phil thought for a moment.

"Give her a call." Annie took her cell phone and dialed. No answer. She shrugged her shoulders.

"Try her again." Annie dialed Mrs. Walsh's phone but still no answer. Annie shook her head.

"She's not there."

"Did family take her?"

"No. And I didn't see her at breakfast." Phil didn't like the sound of that.

"Let's take a walk. Call Hank." They left the dining room and strolled down the corridor as Annie buzzed Hank on her walk-ie-talkie.

"Hank, pick up." Phil and Annie arrived at Mrs. Walsh's front door. Her nameplate beside the door displayed a photo of her with her grandkids. Phil knocked on the door.

"Mrs. Walsh? Are you there?" No answer. Phil grabbed his master key and unlocked the door. They stepped inside. It was fas-tidiously neat and attractive. Family photos hung on the walls.

"Mrs. Walsh? Are you home?" Phil called out. Still no answer. Phil looked at Annie.

"Did you hear something?" Phil said.

"No." She strained to listen. A faint sound came from the bathroom, behind the closed door. Phil approached the door and tapped on it.

"Mrs. Walsh? Are you in there?" From behind the door he heard a faint voice.

"Help. Please help me."

"Oh, my god," Phil muttered. He called out.

"Mrs. Walsh, I'm going to open the bathroom door. Is that OK?" No reply. Phil turned the door knob and inched the door open. It almost immediately struck Mrs. Walsh's back, lying on the floor naked, with a bath towel in hand.

"Mrs. Walsh, you are blocking the door. Can you move?" Hank finally arrived with his work belt strapped to his waist.

"Hank, get a jigsaw. I hate the way they build these doors. We gotta cut the door off its hinges. Annie, call an ambulance."

Mrs. Walsh had gotten out of the tub earlier in the morning and reached for her bath towel when she slipped on the tile floor. She managed to place the towel over her for warmth, and now for modesty.

"You're freezing," Phil said. He looked around and saw her robe hanging on the back of the bathroom door. He helped her put it on.

"Annie, get a blanket." She grabbed a blanket from the bedroom and gave it to Phil, who tucked it around Mrs. Walsh for extra warmth.

"There, you'll be toasty in no time."

"This is so embarrassing," Mrs. Walsh moaned.

"Don't even think about it," Phil said. "How's the view from down there?" Mrs. Walsh smiled at his attempt at humor. Mostly, she was grateful for the rescue.

Parked at the front door of The Sanctuary, the ambulance waited as the EMTs wheeled Mrs. Walsh through the lobby and out the door. Phil followed alongside the gurney, holding her hand as they passed through the front door. Annie and Hank stood ready.

"We called your kids. They're on their way," Annie said.

"I feel so foolish. I just lost my balance. Please don't tell anyone."

"It'll be our secret," Phil said.

"I can't believe you really cut the door off."

"Don't worry. I'm just going to add it to your bill." Her eyes widened. "That was a joke."

The EMTs prepared to hoist Mrs. Walsh inside the ambulance.

"OK – up we go," the EMT called out. Mrs. Walsh gave Phil a look of panic. He smiled.

"I'm coming too," Phil said. After Mrs. Walsh was secured inside, Phil climbed into the back as well. The EMT closed the door. As they whisked away, Phil turned to Mrs. Walsh.

"So, you missed lunch today."

"What did they have?"

"Spaghetti." Back to her old self, she frowned.

"I hate the spaghetti sauce here. It's always too sweet." Phil had to chuckle.

At the emergency room entrance one of the EMTs rolled Mrs. Walsh into the hospital. Phil watched her go.

"I wouldn't worry. She's a tough old broad," the other EMT said. "A lot better shape than the last resident of yours we brought in."

"We got another resident here?"

"Yeah. She's in ICU."

"You're kidding," Phil said. "Show me."

The EMT took Phil to the glass window where he could see Mrs. Ramsey, a frail patient lying in a coma, connected to a spider web of monitors.

"Mrs. Ramsey. We brought her in about six weeks ago, just before Walter retired."

"What the hell happened?"

"Middle of the night she wandered out of her apartment. Hip gave out and she fell flat – landed hard. Been here ever since."

"Unbelievable," Phil said under his breath.

"Sweet old lady. Funny thing is, she never goes anywhere without her walker. But there she was, flat on the carpet with her walker back in her bedroom. Go figure."

Back in the facility, Phil headed straight for Annie's desk.

"Annie, get me Mrs. Ramsey's file." Phil barely got seated at his desk when Annie brought in the file.

"Here it is." Phil opened the file and scanned through it.

"I guess you saw her at the hospital."

"Uh huh." He flipped through the pages and read the incident report. The description of the incident was very brief and explained very little. It basically said she walked out of her apartment at about 2:06 a.m. on March 25 and promptly fell and hit her head.

"This is not much help. What do you know about it?"

"It's kind of a mystery," Annie said. "Mrs. Ramsey is one of our assisted living residents. Real poor balance. Uses a walker all the time. I was told that at two in the morning she left her apartment without her walker for no apparent reason – in her nightgown, no robe, gets about ten feet into the hall and takes a header. The night shift nurse found her in a couple of minutes unconscious. Really sad."

"How's the family taking it?"

"They're pretty upset."

"At us?"

"No. They just don't know why she wasn't using her walker."

"Who was the night nurse?"

"Sylvia Longwood." She pointed to the bottom of the incident report. "See – she is the one who signed the report at the bottom."

"Maybe I should talk to her."

"She doesn't work here anymore. She quit."

"When?"

"The next day."

Allan Dodge worked as head of security for The Sanctuary. He used to work for a computer company and knew the ins and outs of all things electronic. Now, in semi-retirement, he designed all the security features for the facility. He sat at his desk, filing papers, when Phil popped his head in the door.

"Allan, got a minute?"

"Sure. What's up?"

"I need to look at some security footage from six weeks ago."

"Sure, I've got them back here." They walked to the back of his office, where the playback machine sat on a table beside a file cabinet full of discs.

"What do you want to see?" Allan asked.

"I'm trying to follow up on an incident report from March 25. The report said that Mrs. Ramsey was found on the floor in the hallway at 2:06 in the morning."

The two hovered over the playback screen as Allan cued up the disc. He fast forwarded to the early morning hour.

"Let's pick up the action at 2:05," he said, as he slowed the fast forward to a crawl.

"OK. This is it." He hit the STOP button, then pushed PLAY. They watched film footage taken from a mounted security camera in the hallway just down from Mrs. Ramsey's room.

"OK. The camera's down the hall. We'll zoom in on her door," Allan said, as he focused in on Mrs. Ramsey's front door. They watched the action on the screen. The hallway sat empty for several seconds, when suddenly Mrs. Ramsey burst through her front door and hobbled frantically into the hallway in her nightgown. Although there was no audio, the expression on her face clearly registered terror. She mouthed words that could not be heard, then suddenly fell to the ground and struck her head. They watched the screen for several seconds. Phil noticed something.

"Play that back again," said Phil. Allan rewound the action and replayed it. "Did you see that?" Phil said, pointing to the screen.

"What?"

"The time stamp – it jumps about thirty seconds. See? Play it again." They watched the action again and noticed the time stamp skipped thirty seconds shortly after Mrs. Ramsey fell.

"You're right," Allan said. "What the hell. I never noticed that before."

"Somebody messed with the archive," Phil said.

"What for?" Allan said.

"Good question. Who has access to these discs besides you?"

"Just the administrator," Allan said.

# CHAPTER 7

The sun rose on Billings with a glow that bathed The Sanctuary in warm morning light. The sprinklers sent powerful jets of water over the lawn as groundskeepers trimmed shrubs and mulched flower beds. The door to the main lobby elevator opened and Phil stepped out, where Annie intercepted him.

"Here's the list of delinquent rents you asked for," she said as she handed him a file. He scanned the list quickly.

"Anything unusual?" he said.

"Just two that really stand out," Annie said. "Colonel Henjum in 115 and Tom Reese in 185."

"We got a retired colonel here?"

"Yeah – Marine Corps Vietnam vet. His wife just got transferred to the nursing home. His billing is a little bit mixed up right now. No big deal."

"What about this Tom Reese?" Phil said.

"He's really not delinquent. Just a special case," she said. "I'll tell you about him later. Why don't you give the Colonel a visit first. He's a little upset right now about his wife. We sent flowers to the nursing home, but it would be nice if you stopped by."

Phil walked down to apartment 115 and knocked on the door. Joe Henjum answered. He stood straight and lean, a slight gentleman with thinning grey hair and a dignified officer's bearing.

"Col. Henjum?" Phil said, extending his hand.

"Yes, sir," he replied cordially. "And you are?"

"Phil Branson – I'm the new executive director. Trying to get to know everybody."

"Of course – the new post commander. Welcome aboard," Joe said as he gestured for Phil to enter. The Colonel took a seat on his living room couch and offered Phil the lazy-boy stuffed chair. The charming apartment was a bit of a shrine to the Colonel's military life. Framed photos on the wall showcased the Colonel in his dress blues, as well as assorted shots of him with his army buddies. His Marine Corps saber hung mounted on the wall, along with a large framed collection of citations and decorations, including the Purple Heart, Bronze Star, and the Medal of Honor. Phil recognized it right off.

"Col. Henjum, it's an honor to meet you." He pointed to the CMH ribbon. "I've never met a Medal of Honor winner before. Hell of a thing."

"They gave out fifty-seven of those ribbons to Marines in 'Nam – most of them posthumously," Joe said.

"I can't imagine," Phil nodded. Then he noticed the rifle cabinet across the room. It contained a U.S. M16, 12-gauge shotgun, 30-30 Winchester, and various handguns mounted.

"I've never had a resident keep a gun cabinet in his apartment. It's actually against company policy."

"The previous administrator made an exception in my case," Joe said.

"I'm cleaning up a lot of things the previous administrator did."

"I'd greatly appreciate it if you'd allow it."

"You got a license for all of 'em?"

"Yes, sir. I keep them oiled and clean and I go to the gun range once a month. You ever fired a pistol?"

"No. My dad owned one, but I guess I never saw the need."

"Never too late to learn. I'm going to the gun range next week, right here in town. Why don't you join me." Phil gave the invitation a moment of thought.

"You know what – if I'm living out here in the west, I might as well act the part."

"Is that a yes?"

"That's a yes."

"How about the gun cabinet?"

"I guess in your case I'll make an exception. If I can't trust a Medal of Honor winner, then what's the point? Are the guns loaded?"

"No, but I've got ammunition for all of them."

"You expecting trouble?" Phil smiled.

"You never know. Can I get you a drink?"

"I'll have whatever you're having."

"Scotch," Joe said. Phil checked his watch. It wasn't even 10:00 a.m. yet. Hell, he thought, it's 5:00 somewhere.

"One finger," Phil said. As Col. Henjum poured drinks in the kitchen, Phil looked at the photos on the wall. "They look like a bunch of young kids," he said loud enough to reach the kitchen. Henjum returned with two glasses. He handed one to Phil.

"We were. Did you know the average age of a U.S. GI in World War II was twenty-six? In Vietnam it was nineteen." Phil just shook his head and sat back down. He took a courtesy sip.

"You have kids?" Phil asked. Joe nodded.

"Three boys. How about you?"

"No."

"You married?" Joe asked.

"Was – she died in a car accident several years ago back in Orlando."

"Orlando? Then what are you doing out here?"

"I march where orders take me. You know how that goes."

"I sure do." Joe's thoughts strayed to his own wife, and he turned his gaze to her framed picture on the end table beside him.

"I heard about your wife, Mary – heart attack and all. I'm very sorry," Phil said.

"She's in the nursing home now. I'm not much good without

her. It seems everything I care about dies, and I'm always the one left behind."

"Ever been to 'The Wall' in D.C.?"

"No. I don't think I could bear it. Too many names I know," Joe said.

"Might be therapeutic. Closure." Joe's eyes welled up. He raised his glass.

"Here's to the real heroes we left behind." They took a drink. Suddenly Phil's walkie-talkie chirped.

"Phil here," he said. Annie chimed in.

"We've got a, uh, a situation here in the office," Annie said.

"I'll be right down." He turned to the Colonel.

"Duty calls – we'll finish this drink later." He rose to leave, then looked back. "Colonel, thank you for your service."

Phil passed through the administrative work room on his way to his office, where he ran into both Annie and Louisa Martin, one of the laundry workers, visibly irritated.

"Mr. Branson, Louisa Martin, one of our housekeepers, is here to see you." Phil continued into his office.

"Yeah, we've met. Hi, Louisa," he said cheerfully as he walked past her. "Come on in." He took a seat behind his desk as Louisa stormed in, holding an envelope in her hand.

"What is this?" she demanded. Phil extended his hand out to have a look at it. Louisa offered it over.

"This is what the IRS calls a 1099," Phil said, returning the envelope.

"I know what it is – what's it for?" she said.

"Well, you see, wages are taxable no matter what form they are paid in."

"What wages? You didn't pay me any wages."

"As I understand it, for the last four years you and your sister have been receiving free rent in lieu of wages for your laundry services. Now, I'm sure you paid all your withholdings for your imputed income. But still we are required to notify the IRS of the amount you were paid. And that's a two-bedroom apartment you are in, which rents for $3,500 a month. In four years that comes to $168,000."

"I don't have that kind of money," Louisa said.

"I'm sure the IRS will be happy to put you on a payment plan." Louisa knew she had been checkmated.

"What do you want?" she sighed.

"I want your apartment. We just rented it to a lovely couple from Miles City. I need you out by the end of the week."

"The end of the week! Where are we going to live?" Phil ignored that question.

"Now, if you leave on time and the apartment's in good order, and if your work habits from now going forward are commendable, I may just misplace the 1096 that I am required to send to the IRS to inform them of your imputed income."

"We quit," Louisa said.

"Still, you need to be out by Friday. If you're not, we'll just change the locks, box up your things and send them to the good will." Louisa stormed out. Annie popped her head in.

"Mr. Branson, come out here real quick and take a look at this."

"Now what?" Phil thought as he followed Annie to the office window facing the front parking lot.

"What are we looking at?" Phil asked.

"Take a look at that man getting into the car." Phil strained to get a look, but the passenger car door closed before he could see. The car drove off.

"What was I supposed to see?"

"That was Tom Reese."

"Oh, the special case you were talking about?"

"Yes. Once every three months or so he gets picked up by someone who claims he's a friend. They're gone for a couple days, then he comes back."

"So?"

"Just let me bring you his file. You'll see."

# CHAPTER 8

Phil sat down at his desk and opened Tom Reese's file. It showed no previous address, no previous employer, no source of income, no next of kin. Nothing but a single sheet of paper with a contact number.

"Annie," Phil called out. Annie popped her head in the door.

"Yeah?"

"What's this?"

"I thought you'd find that interesting," she said.

"It's all blank. What the hell – why didn't anybody fill this in?"

"The previous administrator took care of it. He said we didn't need to know."

"Know what? We don't let someone just move in unless we do some kind of background check, or at least get an emergency contact for next of kin."

"There is a phone number in there, I guess in case he dies."

"Does he pay his own rent?"

"Well, here's the thing. We get a check every month from a trust account out of New York City. Like clockwork."

"What is he? Some kind of trustafarian?"

"Beats me."

"How long has he been living here?"

"Three years."

"You ever ask Mr. Reese about it?"

"Yeah. He said he'd rather not discuss it. He's very private. But he's no trouble. You hardly know he's here. And his checks always clear, so..."

"Does that beat all? You let me know when he comes back. He's about to become my new hobby."

At the end of the day Phil relaxed in the facility manager's apartment. He read a book on the sofa, with a glass of wine sitting on the coffee table. Late in the evening he heard a knock at the door. Phil checked his watch – 10:30 p.m. He crossed over to the door and opened it. It was Allan, the head of security.

"What's up, Allan?"

"Sorry to bother you, Mr. Branson, but you need to see this."

Phil and Allan entered the outdoor swimming pool area to see the entire deep end filled with the pool loungers that normally lined the pool deck. Obviously, the work of vandals.

"Any idea who did this?"

"Yep." Allan took Phil to the security office where the thirty security cameras around the campus recorded everything that happened day and night, inside and out.

"I cued it up so you could see." He pushed the PLAY button, and the recording presented the entire escapade of Louisa and her sister, two misguided ladies seeking revenge for their eviction. It showed them pitching all the pool loungers into the deep end, all caught on tape. Allan hit the PAUSE button just as Louisa lowered her hoodie and flipped off the camera with her middle finger. Phil shook his head in amazement.

"Wasn't that sweet. Thanks, Allan."

The next morning the facility buzzed with activity as usual, residents and staff crisscrossing through the lobby. Phil breezed through the elevator door on his way to his office. He spotted Fran, the housekeeping director, pushing a cart.

"Hi, Fran. How'd your boy do on his math test?"

"He got an A."

"Good for him." Phil continued to walk past the reception desk.

"Good morning, Tina." Tina was the day shift receptionist, in her early twenties and glad for the job. She treated it as a solemn responsibility. Cute, giggly, and perky, she adored the residents, and they loved her like their own. At any given moment throughout the day, a resident could be seen at the reception desk chatting with Tina about their grandchildren. For them, Tina was considered an honorary grandchild, especially for those who rarely saw their own children. At this moment she was on the phone with a resident, but cupped her hand over the receiver to reply.

"Good morning, Mr. Branson." Then she returned to the call. "Yes, the shuttle bus leaves at 10:00 this morning for the mall. You're welcome, Mrs. Hennessey."

Phil passed through the work room on his way to his office. He spotted Annie at her desk.

"Annie, do we still have that IRS form 1096 for Louisa's imputed income?"

"Yeah – why?"

"Go ahead and drop it in the mail. I'm feeling very civic minded today."

"By the way, Mr. Reese is back – he got dropped off last night."

"Seems like now is a good time to pay him a visit," Phil said, as he rose from his desk.

Tom Reese heard a knock on his front door. He was sixty-eight, with his hair dyed white to age him up even more, and his nose slightly altered, not so much that he was unrecognizable from his earlier life, but hopefully enough to confuse any facial recognition software. He opened the door.

"Yes?" Tom said.

"Phil Branson, I'm the new manager. I think it's time we got acquainted," Phil said. Tom opened the door wider and Phil entered.

Later that morning, Phil rang the doorbell of Walter Angler, the previous administrator. He opened the door.

"Did we have an appointment?" Walter asked.

"No," Phil said.

"Well, what can I do for you? I'm kind of in the middle of something."

"How about we talk about Tom Reese." Walter opened the front door wider and let Phil in the house. Walter sat on the couch across from Phil.

"You didn't clear this with anybody, did you?" Phil said.

"It's better that nobody knows."

"Better for who? Tom or you?"

"Better for everyone."

"How much is the Marshal Service paying you for this?"

"Nothing. Just the rent."

"Is Tom paying you anything under the table?"

"That is definitely none of your business."

"No wonder you retired. Why didn't you just paint a bull's eye on the facility?" Phil said.

"You can't tell anyone. No one. You'll put everybody at risk."

"You already did that yourself, you dumb son-of-a-bitch," Phil said. "Did you think you could keep this a secret forever? Walter! Why here?"

"It was his idea. According to him, this is the middle of no-where – nobody would look for him here."

"When did you stop being a manager?" Walter chose not to reply. "He can't stay. It's too dangerous."

"Leave it alone, Phil."

"Somebody's going to die before this is over. You better pray to God it's not a resident."

"I think it's time for you to leave." They rose and walked to the front door. Phil paused for a moment.

"Oh, one other thing. You know anything about security tapes being tampered with?"

"Of course not. What are you talking about?"

"Mrs. Ramsey, her accident. The security footage looked like it's been altered."

"What are you looking at that for?"

"No reason. Just curious."

After Phil left, Walter got on the phone and made a call to the corporate office to report on Phil's snooping discoveries.

Before returning to The Sanctuary, Phil stopped by the Billings Public Library and found the microfilm room. He searched the drawer for the correct spool of the *New York Times* and fed the film through the reader, then flipped on the light. He wound the spool until he reached the date he was looking for, then slowly scrolled down, searching for the article and photo of the trial of Santino Giovani. He read the article about the other witness who was executed along with Vincent Wallace's wife.

"Damn, they killed his wife," Phil muttered. Then he zoomed in on the picture of Vincent Wallace at the trial. No question about it – Vincent Wallace was Tom Reese.

# CHAPTER 9

The downtown business district of a nondescript city, with mid-rise office buildings, was alive with the usual street traffic and bustling pedestrians. On the fourth floor of an unassuming office complex the elevator opened and a UPS delivery man carrying an express envelope walked down the hallway to an office. He opened the office door and entered. The company name etched on the glass window of the door read "Diamond Enterprises." The UPS man handed the express envelope to Eunice, the receptionist. She was professionally dressed, in her fifties, a veteran of the corporate world. She'd been hired not so much for her secretarial skills as her fierce loyalty and discretion. The lobby was neat and clean. Behind the receptionist desk the company name Diamond Enterprises appeared on the wall in high-relief brushed chrome lettering.

"Sign here." Eunice initialed on the computerized tablet held in place by the UPS man. She handed him back his stylus.

"Thank you." On his way out, the delivery man looked over his shoulder.

"Have a good one." Eunice took the envelope to the inner office door and knocked. She heard the reply from inside.

"Come in." The door to Mr. Diamond's office opened and the receptionist entered with the envelope in hand. She handed it to Mr. Diamond at his desk, who was busy studying a computer screen. The office was decorated with cutting edge furnishings and fixtures.

"This just came."

"Thank you, Eunice." She left the office. Mr. Diamond opened the envelope and scanned its contents. Satisfied, he walked, envelope in hand, to an inner corridor that led to a suite of offices. He called out.

"Conference room – ten minutes."

He stepped into the conference room and set his files down. The room had no windows, but was filled with computer terminals and servers, large flat screen monitors, copy machines, shredders, an encryption machine, a bank of telephones, work tables, chalk boards, storage cabinets, and bookshelves. Other walls held large murals of the United States, Europe, the middle east, and the far east. Another mural highlighted the entire South Pacific. Around the conference table Mr. Packard, a nerdish computer geek, and Mr. Jewel, a lean, bookish type, took a seat.

"We're missing Mr. Stone?" Mr. Diamond said.

"He just called from the parking garage. He's on his way in," Mr. Packard said. The door opened and Mr. Stone entered, pulling his roller board suitcase behind him. He was a mid-twenties rebel in need of a shave and haircut, but dressed in an Oxford shirt and vest. He joined the group at the table.

"Welcome back. How was Dubai?" Mr. Diamond said.

"You gotta love those deposed African dictators. I found this one suffering for his people in a five-star hotel penthouse." The trio snickered and high-fived each other. Mr. Diamond walked over to the chalkboard and taped an eight-by-ten picture of Vincent Wallace's face to the board.

"Well, I agree, that one was easy. But we're going to collect our fee anyway. Let's get back to some real work. We've been retained to find a Mr. Vincent Wallace, former employee of the New York Giovani crime family. He has gone missing for the last three years."

"Can't imagine why," Mr. Jewel said with a chuckle.

"We're not going to get any help from the Marshal Service on this one. No one's talking. I tried, believe me. So, we're going to have to find him the old-fashioned way."

"Where do you want to start?" Mr. Jewel said.

"Mr. Wallace has no wife, but he has two children – Steve, age thirty-nine, and Jennifer, age forty-one, each with children of their own, making Mr. Wallace a proud grandpa. Unless I miss my guess, he's not going to walk away from that. They're his reason for living. So, we are going to start with his children." He held up the express envelope and began dealing out the contents.

"I called in a few favors to collect some essential tracking data. So, here's where we start." He handed a stack of papers to Mr. Packard. "This is all of the banking information on Steve and Jennifer – checking, savings, and investment accounts." He dropped a second pile of papers in front of Mr. Jewel. "These are the telephone records for Steve and Jennifer – land lines and cell phones." He dropped a third pile of papers in front of Mr. Stone. "And these are all of their credit card statements for the past three years." He sat down at the conference table with his trio of expert trackers.

"We are going to see if he has made any contact with his kids in the last three years in any way, shape, or form. Mr. Packard, you're going to look for any unusual banking activity, deposits or withdrawals, bonuses, payments made, routine transactions to or from any mysterious sources. I want to know about every dime coming or going."

"I'm on it."

"Mr. Jewel, I want to know about every phone call they made or received in the last three years – work, social, or otherwise, local and especially long distance. Pay close attention to calls made only once from a particular number, and the time of day. Look for patterns and look for one-offs."

"You got it."

"Last but not least, Mr. Stone, you won't need any sun screen for this. I want to know about their spending habits, particularly credit card travel. I want to know about every place they have been in the last three years, and not just the places they frequent. He's not going to be stupid enough to meet them in the same place twice. Look for any place they went where they had no business being. And that goes for any future trips to unusual places, I want to know the minute they book an airline ticket or a hotel room. When they drive out of state, you're going to track every stop they make."

"No problem. And what about you?" Mr. Stone said.

"I'm going to focus on the internet – e-mail accounts, Facebook, news articles, photos, any key words or phrases in social media that he would use."

"For instance?" Mr. Jewel asked.

"His wife's name was Leora. He may have changed his name, but I doubt he changed hers. That's an unusual name. I'm going to flag that word anywhere it appears in print in every major newspaper and every social media. He's been hiding for three years. He may be getting lazy. He's going to make a mistake, and when he does, we nail him."

# CHAPTER 10

Fresh from a cappuccino run, Phil parked his car in a remote section of the parking lot and walked to the front door. The front entrance was framed by two large terra cotta pots with ornamental shrubbery. The welcome mat looked new with the name of the facility silk screened into it. He stopped and looked at the new sign in front of the reserved parking space. It now read "Employee of the Week." The space was now occupied by a beat-up sedan with a dented side panel. He couldn't help but smile. Phil breezed into the lobby and spotted Hank on a ladder replacing a light bulb in the atrium ceiling.

"Hank," Phil said. Hank looked down from his ladder.

"Yeah, boss?"

"I just wanted to say the front of the building looks terrific. Now, that's curb appeal." Hank gave him a wave. Phil headed toward the office. He paused at the front desk to say hello to the receptionist.

"Hey, Tina."

"Good morning, Mr. Branson."

"So, I noticed that you're the employee of the week," he said. She blushed.

"Oh, yeah. I'm sorry – my car looks like a wreck. I can move it if it's too, you know –"

"Of course not. Enjoy it." Phil turned toward his office, but was intercepted by Annie.

"Mr. Branson, I hate to start your day off with bad news, but Mrs. Ramsey passed away last night." Phil could not hold back a heavy sigh. "The family is coming down. The funeral is going to be on Thursday. I'll take care of sending flowers."

"OK. Thanks. Oh, say, could you get me the move-out history for this facility for the last twelve months?"

"The move-out history?"

"Yes, that's right."

"Sure." Phil retreated to his office and started going through his messages when Annie burst in.

"Mr. Branson, quick, he's here again."

"Who?"

"That fellow who picks up Tom Reese." Phil rose to his feet quickly.

"I thought you said he only comes by every few months."

"I did. I don't know why he's back so soon." Phil headed for the door.

"Well, let's find out."

Tom Reese quietly walked to the front door to leave. He signed out in the resident sign-out clipboard, put on his jacket, and walked out the door to a nondescript late model four-door sedan sitting under the porte cochere, with the engine running, driver waiting. Tom Reese climbed into the passenger seat. The driver put the car in gear when Phil stepped in front of the car to stop it. The driver hit the brakes and reached inside his coat for his service weapon. Tom waved him off.

"No, wait. That's the manager."

Mrs. Cohen was waiting for her ride under the porte cochere when she spotted Phil step in front of the car. She gave Phil a scolding look and wagged her finger disapprovingly.

"Didn't your mother ever teach you to look both ways?" Phil

gave her a sheepish shrug, then slowly walked around to the driver's side and signaled for the driver to roll his window down. The window slowly slid down to reveal Dan Haley, with the U.S. Marshal's Service. He was in his forties, fit, close cropped hair, and plain clothed.

"Can I help you?" Dan said.

"What do you say we all go for a ride and get some coffee?" Phil suggested.

Dan Haley, Tom Reese, and Phil found a picnic table at a local park, each with a cup of coffee. The park sat nearly vacant, with only the periodic jogger and mother with stroller passing by.

"I almost shot you," said Dan.

"I don't think so. That would have spoiled this little secret you got going."

"Listen, I don't know what your game is, but this is Vincent's life you're playing with," said Dan.

"I'm Phil Branson, the new manager of The Sanctuary. I'm assuming you're Tom's handler."

"Dan Haley, U.S. Marshal Service."

"What are you doing here, anyway? I was told you only show up every couple of months."

"There's been a ripple. Someone's pressing the Bureau for Vincent's whereabouts. I don't know why all of a sudden, but someone's pushing really hard."

"Well, who knows besides you?" Phil said.

"The director. That's all."

"I don't like it," Phil said. He turned to Tom.

"I'm sorry, Tom or Vincent, or whatever your name is – but you can't stay at The Sanctuary."

"What do you expect me to do?"

"That's really not my problem," Phil said, then turning back to Dan, "it's yours." Dan turned to Vincent Wallace.

"I told you this wouldn't work."

"Everything was fine for the last three years." Then he turned to Phil.

"I paid your manager a lot of money to stay here."

"Take it up with him. I'm sure he has a refund policy."

"Why can't I stay?"

"Are you kidding? Let me paint you a scenario. You get made and a hit team pays us a visit. You get killed along with, oh, two or three residents who get in the way. We get sued into oblivion and the facility closes down. Something like that."

"All right. I'll make other arrangements," Dan said. "But you gotta give me some time. And you gotta keep quiet about this. Nobody can know. Nobody."

"How much time?" Phil asked.

"A couple of months, at least." Phil rolled his eyes. "I gotta set things up. New home, new back story, new ID. You can't even relocate to the Aleutian Islands without drawing attention. That's what made this setup so sweet."

"Just do it," Phil said, then pointed his finger at Dan's face. "And remember, every time you pull in our driveway, you draw attention." Dan drove Phil back to the facility and dropped him off, then he and Tom drove away. Phil walked back to his office where Annie quivered with curiosity.

"OK, so what's the story? Who is that guy?" she asked.

"I'll tell you about it later. For now just keep cashing his rent checks."

"OK. In the meantime, you might be interested in this." She handed him a direct mail envelope from Whispering Pines Retirement Community.

"What's this?" he said.

"It's a direct mail campaign from one of our competitors targeting this facility."

"How'd you get it?"

"One of our residents gave it to me. They told me just about everyone in the facility got one." Phil opened the envelope and studied the contents.

"They're offering a move-in special for all Sanctuary residents. First six months rent-free and all moving expenses paid," she said. "Does that beat all?"

"I wouldn't worry about it," Phil said. "They used to try that in Florida for a while, till it all backfired."

"Well, I'll just tell you that it's working here."

"Really?"

"Eight residents in the last four months have moved out and moved into Whispering Pines."

"That's not Whispering Pines' fault. That's ours." Annie handed him another file.

"OK. So, here's our move-out history for the past twelve months." Phil gave it a glance.

"We've had a lot of move-outs from people who only lived here a few months. We've got assimilation problems." Then he noticed something odd. "Look at this – we had a move-out at 3:00 in the morning on March 25? That's the same night as the Mrs. Ramsey incident." He turned to Annie. "You believe in coincidences?"

"Sometimes."

"I don't. Get me the file on this move-out."

Phil stopped by the nursing station for the memory care wing, a thirty-room dedicated wing on the first floor. Cindy, a nursing assistant, sat at the station filling out paperwork. She looked up as Phil approached.

"Hi, Mr. Branson."

"Hi, Cindy. I'm looking for the personal care director – Doloris Chastain." Cindy pointed.

"In her office." Phil nodded and walked over. He stood in the doorway to Doloris' office and politely knocked on the door jamb. Doloris looked up from her desk. She was an experienced health care professional, in her fifties, well-groomed and dressed in blue scrubs, the uniform of the department.

"You busy?"

"Not for you. Come on in." Phil sat himself down in a chair across from Doloris. He held a file in his hand.

"Coffee?" she offered.

"No, thanks. I won't take up too much time. I like to get to know each of my department heads a little better. How long you been running personal care here?"

"Oh, going on eight years."

"Before that?"

"Director of nursing over at Beverly Meadows Nursing Home."

"How do you like it here?"

"Couldn't be happier."

"That's good." He cleared his throat. "I got a quick question for you. I was going through the files and saw we had an Alzheimer's resident move out at 3:00 in the morning March 25. A Wilfred Post. Can you explain that?"

"Yeah. Weird, right? I didn't know about it till I came to work the next morning. Mr. Angler, the previous administrator, he called the family in the middle of the night and told them they had to pick up their father."

"At 3:00 in the morning? Why?"

"I never got a straight answer. I know the Alzheimer's wing was full and Mr. Post was living temporarily in the assisted living wing until there was an opening in memory care."

"Is that normal?"

"No. But the family was at their wits end and begged us to take him off their hands."

"So, you just put him in the assisted living wing, then in the middle of the night the administrator wants him gone just like that? I don't get it." Doloris shrugged her shoulders.

"Take it up with him."

# CHAPTER 11

A large gathering surrounded the burial plot for Mrs. Ramsey. The family attended, along with Phil, Annie, and Hank, representing the facility. The minister spoke words of comfort to the mourners. Phil eyed the adult children of Mrs. Ramsey. The son in particular looked more angry than sad. He held a brown paper bag at his side. At the end of the service, the crowd dispersed, and Phil approached the Ramsey family to offer his condolences. He extended his hand to the son, Dale Ramsey. Dale was dark haired, late forties, dressed in a dark suit. His wife Sarah stood beside him.

"Phil, Phil Branson. I'm the new administrator at The Sanctuary."

"Dale Ramsey. My wife Sarah."

"I'm so sorry for your loss. I never met your mother, but everyone at The Sanctuary had good things to say about her."

"Yeah, well..."

"Take all the time you need collecting the things from your mom's apartment. If there's anything I can do..."

"There is one thing."

"What's that?" Dale handed the brown paper bag to Phil. "That was the night gown my mother wore when she fell in the hallway." Phil pulled it out and inspected it. "It was brand new. We gave it to her for her birthday that very day."

"It's very lovely. How'd you get it?"

"I got it from the hospital when she was admitted." Dan pointed to the front of the nightgown.

"Just explain to me one thing. Why is it ripped in the front where the buttons are?" Phil took a closer look.

"I don't know. Maybe she caught it on something when she fell."

"Caught it on what?" Phil folded the nightgown up and returned it to the bag.

"You mind if I hang onto this for a little while?" Phil said.

Phil and Allan cued up the security disc for March 25 to take another look at Mrs. Ramsey's fall. Phil asked Stanley Baker, a speech pathologist from the local speech clinic, to join them. Stanley still wore his white lab coat.

"Allan, this is Stanley Baker, speech pathologist from the speech clinic. Stanley, Allan is our security director." The two shook hands.

"Now, what are we looking for?" Allan asked.

"I want to take another look at Mrs. Ramsey's night gown when she left her room. Stanley, there's no audio, but I want you to see if you can make out what she is saying just by reading her lips."

"OK – I'll try."

"All right. Here we go," said Allan. He hit the PLAY button and they watched as Mrs. Ramsey left her apartment.

"OK. Hit the pause," Phil said. Allan paused the action and they saw a clear rip in Mrs. Ramsey's night gown from the moment she left her room.

"There it is, sure enough," Phil said. "It was ripped before she left the room. All right, hit PLAY." Allan hit PLAY and they watched her anxiously shuffling out her front door. She managed to take ten to twelve steps before she suddenly fell to the ground and struck her head.

"Let me see that again in slow motion. And can you zoom in on her mouth?" said Stanley.

"Yeah, sure." Allan re-cued the action and they studied the incident in slow motion. The extreme zoom rendered the image on the screen somewhat grainy. Just before Mrs. Ramsey took her fall, Stanley called out.

"Freeze it right there." Allan hit the PAUSE button. "She's calling for help."

"Really? How do you know?" Phil said.

"You can tell the words she is forming by the position of her tongue and lips. Look here –" he pointed to the screen. "Right here her tongue is lifted up to her hard palate. There are only four sounds that call for that tongue position – 'D,' 'L,' 'N,' and 'T.' "

"OK. So?" Phil said.

"Right after that, you see that she closes her mouth to form the next sound," Stanley said. "There are only three sounds that begin with the mouth closed – 'B,' 'M,' and 'P.' You can figure it out from there. There are only a few words that you can make from those two letter combinations. The only one that makes sense under the circumstance is 'HELP.' She says it three times. Look."

They re-played the action and watched her mouth as she called out. Stanley provided the vocal, as he lip sync'd her words.

"Help – Help – Help." They stopped the action and stared at each other.

While Phil was learning the finer points of lip reading, Louie Gomer walked through the lobby on his way to visit his mother in apartment 128, with some dry cleaning over his arm. Louie was sixty years old, thinning hair, dressed casual. He helped himself into his mother's front door. She sat on the couch still in her bathrobe, looking very despondent. The TV was on but she paid no attention to it.

"Hi, Mom. I brought your dry cleaning." He hung it in the bedroom closet and returned. "That spot on your sweater –" He suddenly noticed the depressed look on his mother's face. "What's the matter? Are you OK?"

"Why did you move me here?" she asked.

"Why? Is something wrong?"

"Louie, I want to go back home."

"But, Mom, this is your home. We sold your old house two years ago."

"I tried it here like you asked, but I just don't like it. I want to leave."

"What's the matter?"

"It's so full of old people."

"Mom, you're eighty-three years old yourself."

"There's no one to talk to."

"What about at mealtime?"

"That Mrs. Sedgwick woman at my table, she's such a snob. And the lady who sits beside me, she asks me every day what my name is." She cupped her hand to her mouth. "My name is Edith Gomer for the fiftieth time!"

"Mom –"

"I feel like I'm a prisoner here. I don't even have a car anymore."

"Mom, you know you can't drive."

"I can too."

"Your eyesight's bad, your hearing's going, your balance is shot."

"I want my car back."

"We sold it." Mrs. Gomer looked at her son with pitiful eyes, then examined all the wrinkles and veins in her hands. Louie reached for his car keys in his pocket. "Look, mom, we've had this discussion before. Here's my car keys. Let's go for a drive. I'll be the passenger. You drive us to the grocery store and back. You do that and I'll buy you a new car."

"You would not."

"I will." He held out the keys like bait. "Let's go."

"Just go. Leave me alone," she said. She knew he had called her bluff.

"I understand how you feel. I would feel the same way. Your

whole life was invested in raising us kids. Now that Dad's gone and we're all raised and gone, you have no purpose in life. You sit on this couch all day, you never get involved, you haven't made any friends. I'd be depressed too."

"I just want to die," she said softly.

Phil just walked Stanley out and thanked him, when Annie took him aside.

"Got a minute?"

"Sure. What's up?"

"Mrs. Gomer's son is here. Wants to talk."

"Mrs. Gomer?"

"One-twenty-eight. Sweet lady. Kind of a recluse." Phil nodded and asked Annie to let him in. Louie Gomer entered the office. Phil rose and crossed over to greet him.

"Phil Branson. Have a seat."

"Louie Gomer. Thanks." He sat down across from Phil's desk. "I hate to bother you. If you're busy –"

"No, not at all. What's up?"

"It's my mother. She is majorly depressed. I don't know what to do. I think she might be suicidal."

The heartfelt meeting lasted for several minutes. At its close they both exited Phil's office. Louie shook his hand and left. Phil turned to Annie.

"Annie, I need you to print up a help wanted poster."

"OK."

"Only residents who have lived here at least two years need apply. The job title is Move-In Coordinator. Whoever takes the job will get a rent discount."

"Got it."

"But don't post it. Just give it to me when you finish making it." With that, Phil started to walk out the door.

"Where you going?"

"Gonna see a man about a horse. Oh, while I'm gone, pull up our phone records for last March."

# CHAPTER 12

Phil pulled into the parking lot of Whispering Pines Retirement Community, one of his competitors in Billings. It was a large resort style community with a handsome community center, attractive landscaping, and excellent curb appeal. Phil walked in the front door and stepped up to the receptionist. The lobby was attractive, with its western theme paintings and sculptures. A baby grand piano sat at one end of the lobby, where a guest pianist played classic western tunes. Right now he was transforming "The Navaho Trail" into a lovely instrumental. A small gathering of residents sat around the piano, enjoying the music.

"May I help you?" the receptionist said. Phil handed her his business card.

"Yeah, Phil Branson here to see your administrator."

"Did you have an appointment?"

"No. Just a courtesy call." The receptionist picked up the phone and spoke to the other end for a moment.

"He'll be right out," she said. Phil nodded and turned around to take in the ambiance. He sensed a good warm feeling in the air. Furnishings and fixtures were top notch, residents came and went. The lobby seemed open and inviting. John Howard emerged from the office to greet Phil. He was in his thirties, handsome, aggressive, in business dress and western boots.

"Phil Branson – I was wondering when you would pay us a

visit. Come to check out the competition?"

"Yeah, I need to see how the other side lives." They shook hands.

"John Howard. I've been running this cattle drive here going on five years now. Welcome." He led Phil to his office, which emoted a distinctly western flavor, with western paintings and a set of longhorns mounted on the wall. Phil made himself comfortable.

"Can I get you anything? Water? Coffee? Whiskey?"

"Water would be fine." John lifted a bottled water from his small refrigerator and tossed it to Phil, then sat at his oversized desk.

"So, you're Walter's replacement."

"Yep."

"He was a good guy. We worked well together. Traded information, rental rates, employees."

"Even residents?" John offered a nervous chuckle. "What do you mean?"

"Oh, I just noticed that eight of our move-outs in the last four months came over here to live. And last week I saw your shuttle bus parked in our driveway loading up some of our residents." John saw no need to defend himself. He smiled nervously. "You wouldn't be stealing residents, now, would you?"

"Hey, it's not my fault if they're not happy over at your place."

"Unhappy is one thing," He pulled out a direct mail envelope. "But you've been targeting our facility with a direct mail campaign offering deep discounts and free move-in assistance. That's pretty cold-blooded."

"Hey, Phil, don't take it personal. There's six retirement communities in Billings, and I'm an equal opportunity scavenger. That's how we stay full."

"I don't know how the other facilities feel, but the next time your shuttle bus pulls into our driveway, you better be bringing us our dry cleaning."

"Phil, c'mon. Everybody does it."

"No, they don't. This is a small town. You keep it up, and you're going to be a lonely guy."

"I didn't take this job to make friends with the competition." Phil stood to leave.

"Johnny, here's a little secret. The other retirement centers in Billings – we're not your real competition."

"If they're not, then who is?"

"If you don't know, you got no business running this place."

When Phil got back to The Sanctuary, Annie handed him the "help wanted" poster she just prepared.

"Here you go. Is that what you had in mind?" Phil held the poster up at arm's length for a look-see.

"Yeah. That'll do. Thanks." As Phil turned to go back to his office, he heard a thunder of applause from everyone in the lobby. He turned to see what the celebration was about and saw Mrs. Walsh entering the front door using a walker, with the help of her daughter. She blushed at the greetings and affection, as they all took turns hugging her. Annie joined in the hug-fest.

"Welcome back. We missed you," Annie said. One of the housekeepers came over.

"Mrs. Walsh, it's so good to see you," one of the nursing assistants joined in. "Let me give you a hug. You look so good. How are you feeling?"

"Much better, thank you."

"She didn't break anything. Just got banged up," her daughter said. "They just kept her in rehab for a while to make sure she got her balance back." The nursing assistant pulled out her cell phone to take a picture.

"Everybody get together for a picture. We gotta put it in the newsletter." A cluster of well-wishers pressed around Mrs. Walsh and the nursing assistant snapped a shot. Mrs. Walsh felt overwhelmed at the warm greeting. Using her walker, she and her daughter strode down the hall. Mrs. Walsh noticed Phil smiling and gave him a nod.

Phil took the help wanted poster down to Mrs. Gomer's apartment. He found her sitting on her couch staring out the window.

He sat down beside her on the couch and showed her the poster.

"I can't wait any longer. The application deadline is today," he said.

"What are you talking about?"

"This position I'm trying to fill. We've had this poster on the bulletin board for the last three weeks."

"I must not have noticed. Move-in coordinator? Why are you telling me about it?"

"Are you kidding? I was told you'd be perfect for the job."

"Me? I'm just a resident."

"I wouldn't trust this job to anyone else."

"I don't understand."

"We've been noticing that residents are moving in here, then after about two or three months they decide they don't fit in and they move out. That's our fault for not making them feel welcome. Listen, I'll never fill this place up if we move in four then turn around and lose four the same month."

"Well, what am I supposed to do?"

"You remember how scared you were when you first moved in here? All the questions you had? Whether you'd make any friends? Who you'd eat with in the dining room?"

"Yes."

"Wouldn't it have been nice if a resident had knocked on your door your first day and asked you to join her for dinner?"

"Yes."

"We need a seasoned resident to make new move-ins feel welcome. Help them find their way around. Check on them, take them to the bingo game. Invite them over to your apartment for tea. You know, break the ice."

"Why me?"

"I checked your file. You were a high school teacher before you retired. You won awards. You can recall those new freshmen students who were total strangers and scared to death, can't you?"

"Yes. I always tried to make them feel welcome."

"Exactly. That's exactly what we need here."

"I don't know."

"I'm prepared to reduce your rent in half in exchange for your skills in making new residents feel a part of the community."

"It's that important to you?"

"Every resident you keep from leaving saves us $50,000 a year. Honestly, if you don't help me solve this, I don't know what we'll do."

"I'm ashamed to admit it, but I was thinking of leaving myself." Phil noticed a Bible sitting on the coffee table.

"Are you a religious person, Mrs. Gomer?"

"Yes. Baptist." Phil picked up the Bible and turned to the Book of Esther.

"You recall the story of Queen Esther, the Jewish girl who rose to become the queen of Persia."

"Yes. Why?"

"When she learned of a plot to kill all the Jews in the kingdom, her uncle Mordecai, begged her to plead for the lives of her people. But she was afraid to approach the king with such a request. You remember what Mordecai told her?"

"No, what?" Phil found the text in scripture.

"He said, 'Who knows that perhaps you came to this position for just such a moment as this.'"

Mrs. Gomer felt a wave of peace wash over her.

# CHAPTER 13

Phil got back to the office and called Annie in.

"We got a new Move-In Coordinator."

"Who?"

"Mrs. Gomer. We got a spare office we can give her?"

"I think I can find one." She smiled. "That was very sweet of you."

"That was strictly business. She's going to help us stop that revolving door."

"Whatever you say. By the way, here are those phone records from last March." She handed him the file.

"Good. Thanks."

At the end of the day Annie closed up her office to go home. She noticed Phil sitting alone in the far corner of the dining room studying the phone records file. She looked at her watch – 7:45 p.m. She walked over to check on him.

"How you doing?" she asked. He closed the file.

"This place is a mess. Why do you still work here?"

"I guess I was just waiting for the cavalry to arrive."

"I think I know how General Custer felt – outmanned, outgunned."

"I think you are doing a great job so far."

"We got bigger messes here than I can ever untangle."

"Like what?"

"The usual management screw-ups, but some stuff that's off the charts bad."

"How bad?"

"End of world bad."

"Can you talk about it?"

"I wish I could. But I can't."

"You're not going to quit on us, are you?"

"No. I got too much invested. I guess I'll just go down with the ship."

"Is there any hope for us?"

"I don't know. Honest to God, I don't know."

The next morning at staff meeting, Phil made an announcement.

"Final item. We have a new position here at The Sanctuary. Move-In Coordinator. Mrs. Edith Gomer has accepted our offer and will be starting today. She will be a one-person welcome committee for all new residents. It'll be a handful, and she may need some help with each of you department heads, especially you, Susan, in marketing. So, let's make ourselves available. Any questions?" No response. "OK, then. We're at eighty percent occupancy. That's great news. You're all doing a great job. Let's go get'em."

The meeting adjourned and the staff returned to their assignments. Annie approached Phil.

"Louie Gomer is waiting for you in your office."

"OK. Thanks." Phil got to his office to find Louie Gomer waiting, seated across from Phil's desk. Louie rose to greet him.

"Louie, hope you didn't wait too long."

"No, no problem. I just have one question – what did you do?"

"What do you mean?"

"I came in this morning to see my mom and she blew me off, said she was too busy. I haven't seen her this way in years."

"I guess I made her an offer she couldn't refuse."

"Whatever you did, you saved my life. You saved her life."

"With any luck, she'll save us all. C'mon – I'll walk you out."

Phil and Louie entered the lobby from the administrative office just in time to see Mrs. Gomer, with clipboard in hand, touring a new resident. As she pointed out the features of the lobby, she caught a glimpse of her son and waved. Phil pat Louie on the back and sent him on his way. Back in his office, Phil continued to muse over the mystery of Mrs. Ramsey leaving her apartment and calling for help. Suddenly an idea came to him.

Phil and Allan went back to the screening room, cueing up the footage from the night of March 25.

"OK, boss, what are we looking for now?"

"Up until now we've only been interested in seeing what happened when Mrs. Ramsey left her apartment. We never even thought about what happened before she left."

"What are you thinking?"

"I'm trying to figure out why she ran out calling for help. Let's cue the footage to 1:30, a half hour before she came out."

"OK." Allan fast forwarded the disc to 1:30 a.m., then hit PLAY.

"Go ahead and speed up the action," Phil said. Allan ran the tape fast forward. They watched until the time stamp skipped.

"Wait. Stop. Did you see that? Go back. We've got another skip in the time stamp," Phil said. Allan backed up the disc to 1:53. He replayed the footage at normal speed. At 1:55:10 the time stamp skipped thirty seconds and jumped to 1:55:40. They looked at each other in amazement.

"I'll be damned. Somebody erased footage before and after she fell," Allan said.

"It's time I had a talk with somebody," Phil said.

In the afternoon Phil walked up to the front door of Sylvia Longwood's home, the night nurse who witnessed the Mrs. Ramsey incident. The neighborhood where she lived was sketchy and her humble dwelling looked like a strong wind might blow it down. The front porch was scattered with toys and a rusty old bicycle. Phil rang the doorbell. From inside, he heard a voice.

"Who is it?"

"Phil Branson, from The Sanctuary."

"What do you want?" she asked from behind the closed door.

"I need to clear up a few things about Mrs. Ramsey."

"What sort of things?"

"Did you know she passed away last week?" The door slowly opened a crack and Sylvia peered out at Phil, clearly shaken by the news. She was dark haired, in her thirties, average weight and height.

"I, I didn't know that. I'm so sorry." Phil heard another voice behind the door.

"Who is it, Mommy?"

"It's just a man from work," she said to her son. Then she spoke to Phil.

"That's my son. His father doesn't live here anymore."

"I understand."

"Who are you again?"

"Phil Branson. I took over for Mr. Angler at The Sanctuary. Would you mind if I just came in for a few minutes? I'm really fuzzy on what exactly happened that night."

"I can't. I need to take Jimmy to the babysitter and then get to work."

"Where do you work now?" Phil asked.

"Tip Top Home Health Care."

"It won't take long. Really," Phil said.

"I already explained it in the incident report. There's really nothing else to say."

"You didn't say anything about Wilfred Post." The fact that Phil knew that name stunned Sylvia.

"Why? What – what do you mean?"

"You tell me."

"I really have to go. I don't know anything," Sylvia said.

"She fell in the hallway at 2:06. Somebody made a call to Chicago at 2:30. Was that you?"

"No. Why would I do that? Now, please Mr. Branson, I have to go." She backed away and closed the door. Phil thought for a moment.

"If you ever feel like talking, call me. You know – call the facility." He slipped her his business card through the crack in the door and waited for a reply. Hearing none, he left.

In her living room Sylvia sat nervously on the couch, fighting back a wave of dread. She picked up the phone and dialed. In Walter's living room the phone rang.

"Hello?"

"Mr. Angler, this is Sylvia."

"Sylvia, is everything all right?"

"No. A Mr. Branson just came to see me. He's asking questions about Mrs. Ramsey. He knows."

"He doesn't know anything. Just calm down."

"No. He asked about Wilfred Post. I know he knows. I can't keep lying. What do I do?"

"Just go to work like you always do, and relax. Let me worry about Mr. Branson. Say hello to Jimmy for me. I know how important your little boy is to you. We'll talk again."

Walter hung up and thought for a moment, then dialed a new number.

"Yes?"

"This is Walter – I think you better get out here." Darryl Brooks did not immediately reply. When he heard Walter hang up from his end, he slowly returned the receiver to its cradle and pondered for a moment.

Just before dinner at the Walter Angler house, the doorbell rang. Clara's hands were full in the kitchen, and she called out to her husband.

"Dear, would you get that? I'm grilling onions." Walter opened the front door to find Phil standing on his front porch stoop.

"Who is it?" Clara called out.

"It's Phil Branson."

"See if he'd like to stay for dinner." Without even asking, Walter called back.

"No, he can't stay." Then Walter turned to Phil. "What do you want?"

"There's no scenario where this turns out good for The Sanctuary," Phil said.

"Are we talking about Tom Reese?"

"I'm talking about Mrs. Ramsey."

"An unfortunate accident. Nothing more."

"Did the police investigate this?"

"Yeah, they took a look, but it was nothing, just a trip-and-fall. Happens all the time – you know that."

"What did you edit out of that surveillance footage?"

"Phil, this is not your job description. You just think about what you're doing."

"Why did you have Wilfred Post removed from the facility at 3:00 in the morning?"

"He was disruptive. He didn't belong in the assisted living wing."

"What were you doing up at 3:00 in the first place?"

"I got a call from the night nurse."

"And why did you call Chicago at 2:30?"

"Phil. Walk away. Whatever you're thinking, whatever little theories are rolling around in your brain are only going to end in lawsuits. Just go back to managing the facility before you end up getting the place closed down. How would the residents benefit from that?"

"Say hello to your wife for me," Phil said as he turned and left.

The wheels in Phil's brain churned feverishly as he drove back to The Sanctuary. When he arrived, he knew he needed some sage advice.

Col. Henjum sat glued to the history channel, engrossed in a program on gas warfare during World War I. He heard a knock at the door. He put the TV on mute to see who it was.

"Mr. Branson, please come in," Joe said.

"I don't want to bother you, but I could sure use some help," said Phil.

"Let's sit down." They moved to the couch. "You look like you need a drink."

"I probably do. Maybe four or five drinks – later. I got a question for you – hypothetical."

"OK."

"Suppose someone in your unit created conditions that led to the death of one of your men, then covered it up. He may have done it to protect his own skin, or he might have tried to protect the Corps from loss of face. Either way, he buried the truth. What would you do?"

"And how did I learn about this?"

"You just pieced it together after the fact."

"Son, at the end of the day there's this essential thing called the code of honor. It's not flexible. It's not optional. It's the thing you follow if you're going to live with yourself."

"Even if the Corps takes a hit?"

"It's not your job to save the Corps. It's big enough to take care of itself."

"But a lot of people are going to get hurt."

"Yeah, I know. In my line of work I saw a lot of death. Some of it was deserved and some of it wasn't. You can't control everything. But you gotta look in the mirror and like what you see."

# CHAPTER 14

Phil realized that playing detective was not his strong suit. He knew he didn't have all the facts, and without any evidence or proof, he could end up being sued for going public with unprovable allegations. He cooled his jets for a few days and got back to the business of running The Sanctuary. At lunch he enjoyed mingling with the residents in the dining room. He spotted Mrs. Walsh, who waved him over.

"How you doing, Mrs. Walsh," Phil said. She smiled and pointed to her shrimp cocktail.

"Six shrimp – I've got six shrimp in my cocktail. Thank you," she said.

"And how's your hot water?"

"Boiling," she grinned. "It's so hot I could make tea with it."

"Glad to hear it," he said, as he moved on to other tables.

Sylvia sat watching TV with her son when they heard the doorbell ring.

"Stay where you are," she said, then went to the door and called out.

"Who is it?"

"Walter – Walter Angler." She turned to Jimmy.

"Jimmy – go to your room for a few minutes."

"But what about my show?"

"Just do as I say." In a huff, Jimmy complied. When he was out of sight, Sylvia opened the door to reveal both Walter Angler and Darryl Brooks.

"Hello, Sylvia. I thought we might have a few words with you. This is Darryl Brooks. He's the director of operations for United Senior Living."

"Hello, Sylvia," Darryl said. "Can we come in?" Sylvia reluctantly opened the door wide to let them in. They both helped themselves to the living room couch. Sylvia sat on the stuffed chair beside the couch.

"What a lovely home you have here," Darryl said.

"Thank you."

"Sylvia, I could tell by your phone call to me that you were concerned over the Mrs. Ramsey incident," Walter said.

"You know she died?"

"Yes, we know," said Darryl.

"What am I going to do? Could I go to jail?"

"Yes, you could. That's why we're here. We're trying to protect you," Darryl said.

"I can't go to jail. What about Jimmy?"

"No – we won't let you go to jail. But you can't talk to anybody about what happened that night," Darryl said.

"But that new administrator, Mr. Branson, it seems like he knows everything."

"No, he doesn't know anything. If he did, he wouldn't have come by asking you questions," Walter said.

"It just seems like we should just tell what happened. You know, everything."

"No, we can't do that now. There are people who would love to sue us and to sue you. You don't want that to happen. You didn't mean for Wilfred to go in her room. You should have been watching him, but you were busy taking care of another resident," Darryl said.

"We're on your side," Walter added. "But others might not see it that way. They want to blame somebody. And unfortunately, they're going to blame you," Walter said.

"If you just stay quiet, this will all go away. In the meantime, are you comfortable here? Is there anything you need?" said Darryl.

"I have a night job, but I could use some help with baby-sitting Jimmy. It gets expensive."

"Not a problem. We'll help you with that," Walter said.

"OK. Now, what if the police show up? What do I say to them?"

"You don't say anything. You found her on the floor. That's all you know. Understand?" said Darryl.

"I don't see how this is going to work. I'm not a good liar. They're going to know."

"You won't be lying if you just say what you saw," Walter said.

"But I saw Mr. Post leave her apartment."

"You don't know what happened in that apartment – all you know is Mrs. Ramsey tripped and fell. You found her on the floor," Water said. Sylvia nodded in agreement.

"All right, then. We'll be in touch. If you need me for anything, just call. And do not talk to Mr. Branson. Just send him to me," Walter said.

"OK."

The two let themselves out. Once in the car, they turned to each other.

"What do you think?" Walter said.

"I don't like it. She could put us all in jail."

"What do we do?" Walter asked.

"We have to make sure she doesn't talk. Ever."

A week later Phil sat in his manager's apartment sipping coffee and reading the obituaries. It was an old habit he learned from his early days as an assistant administrator. His boss, Bob Summers, once told him that the obituaries were an excellent source of new customers – not the deceased, but the surviving spouse. As it was explained to him, when an aging husband dies, the widow is often ready to sell that big empty house and make a change. If you played your cards right you might just convince her to move into your community. It is no surprise that eighty percent of all retirement community apartments are occupied by widows.

As he casually scanned down the page, one name jumped out at him – Sylvia Longwood, the nurse's aide who found Mrs. Ramsey in the hallway. Suddenly he felt like he'd been hit by a truck. He read the article on her passing. The cause of death was listed as a drug overdose. He became livid. More like murder by overdose, he thought. She was no druggie – he'd seen enough to know. She was a hard worker and a dutiful mother of a young boy. No way she was hooked on drugs. Now he understood the stakes in the Ramsey case – life or death and winner takes all.

# CHAPTER 15

Phil stood among a modest collection of friends and family for the graveside service of Sylvia Longwood. Some of her co-workers joined, as did church and school friends from the past. A particularly bereft elderly woman in black laid a flower on the casket and fought back tears as she sat down. Beside her was Jimmy, Sylvia's young son, and another woman about Sylvia's age, holding Jimmy's hand. Phil scanned the faces of the rest of the group and spotted Walter Angler standing near the back. Phil stepped back and joined Walter.

"Nice of you to come," Phil said.

"I felt I owed her that much."

"I read the obituary – drug overdose?" Phil said.

"A shame. Just a shame. I had no idea," Walter said.

The minister offered up the usual hopeful words about that great resurrection day when the dead in Christ shall rise. Sylvia's friends and loved ones shared their profound heartache at this senseless loss to her mother, and respectfully dispersed. Phil could not think of any words that would bring comfort to the family, and turned to leave. A young woman in black approached him.

"Are you Mr. Branson?" she asked.

"Yes. I saw you holding little Jimmy's hand. Are you part of the family?" Phil said.

"I'm her sister – Darlene."

"I didn't know she had a sister, but I only spoke to her once or twice."

"She told me about you."

"She did?"

At that moment Walter helped himself over to this private graveside conversation.

"I couldn't help but notice you during the service," Walter said. "Were you close to the deceased?"

"I guess you could say that," Darlene said.

"I'm Walter Angler – Sylvia worked for me over at The Sanctuary."

"I know – I've seen you before." Walter nodded and waited for their conversation to continue, but Darlene fell strangely silent.

"Well, I hope I didn't intrude," Walter said.

"I was just leaving," Darlene said. She turned in the direction of her car.

"I guess I'm done here, too," Phil said. He peeled away and made his way to his car. Walter decided there was nothing more to do or say, and parted company as well.

Phil unlocked his car door and was about to get in, when Darlene appeared, more anxious than ever.

"Mr. Branson," she whispered sharply.

"Darlene – what's wrong?" She looked to the left and right.

"I didn't want to talk to you in front of Mr. Angler." Again she searched for the whereabouts of Walter. "I've got something for you." He saw she held a large envelope.

"Sylvia was no drug addict," she began. "She was scared for her life."

"From who?"

"Walter."

"Did he threaten her?"

"He forced her to lie about something at work to save his neck. Then he threatened her boy. She didn't know what to do. She came to me one night and gave me this envelope and said if she disappeared or was found dead, I was to give this to you."

"Why me?"

"She figured you'd know what to do with it." She handed the large nine by twelve-inch brown envelope to Phil.

"So, here it is. Whatever she got mixed up in, it got her killed. If this is what got her killed, I don't want it. And if I were you, I'd be careful who you showed this to. But if you can clear her name, I would appreciate it." She turned quickly and left.

Phil did not dare open the envelope just yet. He tossed it in the car, looked around to be sure he was alone, then drove back to The Sanctuary.

Late afternoon he settled in his apartment. He sat the envelope on the kitchen table and poured himself a glass of wine. He drank a few sips and stared at it for several minutes. Then he opened it.

Annie's cell phone rang.

"This is Annie."

"This is Phil. Are you busy?"

"No. What do you need?"

"I'm in my apartment. Would you come up here? I've got something I need to show you."

"You can't bring it down here?"

"I'd rather not just yet."

"OK, I'll be right up."

"Don't tell anyone where you're going. I know this sounds weird. Just trust me."

She walked to the elevator and pushed the button to the third floor, got out and made her way to the end of the hallway, and knocked on his door. He quickly opened it.

"C'mon in," he waved her in and quickly closed the door behind her.

"What's going on?" she asked. He directed her to the kitchen table where the envelope sat.

"I got this from Sylvia's sister at the funeral today. Take a look inside." She sat down and opened the envelope's flap and pulled out three pieces of paper, then studied them for a moment.

"OK, they're incident reports from our assisted living wing."

"Look who signed them."

"Sylvia Longwood," Annie said.

"Read them," Phil said. She did. It took a few minutes for the contents to fully sink in.

"Oh, my god," her mouth dropped open. The first incident report was dated March 11. It recorded an altercation between Wilfred Post and Mrs. Solomon. According to the report, Wilfred broke into her apartment and tried to attack her. Due to his feebleness and general confusion, she managed to unhand him and raced out of her unit to the nursing station. He was subdued by staff and returned to his apartment. The nurse on duty filled out the report, signed it, and filed it.

The second incident report was dated March 15. Again, Wilfred barged into another apartment late at night, this time Mrs. Cheavers', and attempted to force her onto her bed. She fought him off and ran from the bedroom, closing the door behind her. Again, the late-night staff redirected Wilfred to his own apartment and filed the incident report. Walter Angler was notified, who made a few calls, then instructed the assisted living personnel to keep a closer eye on Wilfred.

The third, and most incriminating report dated March 25 – the Mrs. Ramsey incident. This report summarized events surrounding Mrs. Ramsey's escape and fall. Again, Wilfred Post gained access to her apartment around 2:00 a.m. There were no cameras recording the activities that transpired inside her apartment, but shortly after 2:00 she ran from her unit and down the hallway, wearing a torn nightgown. There she tripped and fell, striking her head and losing consciousness. Sylvia filled out this report, and specifically noted that Wilfred Post exited her apartment while she was still rendering aid to the fallen Mrs. Ramsey.

"This is devastating," Annie said.

"Why aren't these reports on file?" Phil asked.

"I've never seen these before," Annie said. "There's no report on file for the Mrs. Solomon and Mrs. Cheavers incident. And the one incident report we have for Mrs. Ramsey said nothing about Wilfred Post."

"Show me," Phil said. Annie returned to the office and grabbed the Ramsey file, which contained the incident report, and took it upstairs to Phil's apartment.

"Here it is," Annie said. Phil studied the report from the Ramsey file, which said nothing about Wilfred Post. He compared it to the report from the envelope delivered by Darlene.

"Look at this – both reports were signed by Sylvia, but the signatures are different," Phil said. "One of them is obviously a forgery. Shouldn't take long to figure out which."

"And what about these other two reports. Those reports don't even exist in our regular files," Annie said.

"Obviously, somebody removed them when nobody was looking," Phil said. "I wonder who?"

"Well, Mrs. Solomon and Mrs. Cheavers still live here, so we can interview them again and get their story on record," Annie said.

"I'll handle that in the morning," Phil said. "But one piece of evidence that's still missing is the proof that Wilfred was in her room. The security footage was altered. Somebody erased the film showing Wilfred entering and leaving her room." They both thought for a moment.

"Both cameras?" Annie asked.

"What do you mean 'both?'"

"Mrs. Ramsey's apartment is at the intersection of two hallways. One hallway 'T's' right in front of her front door, but the other hallway…" Annie said, but Phil caught her meaning right away and interrupted her.

"You're right, it runs right past her door and on down past another twenty or so apartments."

"And there's a separate security camera at the end of that hall that records everything that happens along that hallway," Annie said.

"Thanks, Annie. I'll take it from here." They both left the apartment – Annie returned to her office and Phil went directly to Allan Dodge's office. Annie felt flush from the excitement of this bit of sleuthing detective work. She never participated in solving a crime before, and this made her feel very essential. Walter never included her in any consequential matters. In fact, on more than one occasion he urged her to mind her own business. Now she was starting to see why. Phil, quite the contrary, welcomed her input, which not only validated her sense of worth, but also drew her closer emotionally to Phil.

"Allan, got a minute?" Phil said, as he popped his head in Allan's office.

"What do you got?" Allan said.

"I want to look at another tape from March 25," Phil said.

"Which one?"

"The one from the north hallway, the one that passes by Mrs. Ramsey's door, not the one that terminates at her door."

"You're right. I hadn't thought about that one," Allan said. He went to the scanner and loaded the disc from the north hallway, and advanced it to 2:00 a.m. March 25.

"OK, let's run it in real time," Phil said. "And see if you can enlarge the picture." They stood staring at the screen for a minute when they saw Wilfred Post appear from the intersecting hallway and enter Mrs. Ramsey's unit.

"Did you see that?" Phil said, pointing at the screen.

"I'll be damned," Allan said. They continued watching the vacant hallway for about five minutes, when Mrs. Ramsey emerged from her room and hobbled as quickly as she could away from her front door. In a flash she disappeared into the intersecting hallway, and they lost sight of her. They continued watching as Sylvia responded to her cry for help, turning into the hallway where Mrs. Ramsey lay. In another minute Wilfred emerged from Mrs. Ramsey's door and shuffled down the hallway.

"Make me a copy of that," Phil said.

# CHAPTER 16

The next morning at staff meeting, Susan reported the new move-ins.

"That puts us at eighty-two percent now," she beamed. Phil initiated the applause.

"That's terrific," he said. Then turning to the rest of the group. "Food service, I really like what you did with the rotisserie chicken yesterday. What did you do?"

"We tried a new glaze," the food service director said, smiling.

"Well, that was a winner. Keep it up."

At the end of the meeting, Phil cornered Doloris Chastain.

"Can we chat in your office when you have a minute?" he asked. Doloris looked at her watch.

"I'm meeting with a family that's waiting in the lobby. How about at 9:30?"

"I'll be there," Phil said. Susan approached Phil with a question.

"Mr. Branson, I know we still have about forty more apartments to rent, and those are gonna be the toughest ones, in the worst locations. But we have five units on the ground floor that are all in prime spots, but they're being used for storage right now. If you could get them cleared out, I could rent them tomorrow."

"I'll get on it today," Phil said. He found Hank in the laundry room overseeing the repair of one of the industrial washers.

"Can I borrow you for a minute?" Phil asked.

"Sure," Hank said. They walked down the ground floor hallway to units 45-49. Phil opened the door to unit 45, revealing rows of mattresses stacked up in the living room, with the metal frames organized in the bedroom.

"Don't we have any facility storage for this?" Phil asked.

"No – they didn't even think about storage when they built this place. It's a problem. I've got some storage sheds out back for the lawn equipment and stuff, but we got no place for furniture, Christmas decorations, files, and such."

"We got resident storage that we rent by the month – any extra space there?"

"Every storage bin is being used, and the fire Marshal has warned us about keeping walkways clear, so I can't just cram more stuff in there."

"Understood. We'll have to rent some off-site storage space for our overflow. We can't be using rentable space for mattress storage. We're losing $10,000 a month by taking those five units offline. That will pay for a helluva lot of off-site storage."

"You're right."

"Get it done today," Phil said. "No rush or anything," he added.

Phil sat waiting in Doloris' office. He checked his watch – 9:35. He saw her breeze in, full of apologies.

"So sorry – took longer than expected. One of our ladies is going to start needing insulin shots, and we had to work that out with the family." She set her files on her desk and sat down. "Now, what can I do for you?" Phil handed her the three incident reports he received at the funeral.

"Do any of these look familiar?" She scanned all three. Her face turned sober.

"Where'd you get these?"

"Do you have copies of these in your file?" Phil asked.

"Well, I don't see why not."

"Check and see, if you don't mind."

"Now?"

"I'll wait," Phil said. Doloris slowly rose from her desk and went to the file cabinet. She skimmed down the rows of resident files. First, she stopped at Mrs. Cheavers. She pulled out her file, then flipped down to Mrs. Solomon and pulled her file. Finally, she pulled Mrs. Ramsey's file and brought the three over to her desk.

"Let's just have a look," she said. She slowly opened Mrs. Cheavers' file and skimmed through the papers. "I don't see this incident report in her file," Doloris admitted. Phil started boring in.

"Why wouldn't it be there?"

"Either that report is a fake, or somebody pulled the report out."

"While I was waiting for you, I stopped by Mrs. Cheavers and Mrs. Solomon, and they both confirmed that these invasions occurred. So that eliminates the 'fake' option." He could see that Doloris was becoming more uncomfortable by the second. "Their version of events paints a pretty dark picture. Luckily, they didn't get hurt, but Mrs. Ramsey died." Doloris became more agitated.

"That was just an accident."

"I'm afraid not – security footage says otherwise." Doloris pulled the Ramsey file out. She found the incident report and showed it to Phil.

"But that's not what her incident report says." Phil handed her the incident report given to him at the funeral.

"Look at his one. It tells a different story. And you want to talk about fakes. Compare the signatures on these two reports. They don't match. That means somebody else signed this form instead of Sylvia. You wouldn't know anything about that, would you?" Doloris put on her most indignant face.

"Certainly not. And I'll thank you to hand these reports over so I can put them in their files."

"You can make copies if you like, but I'm hanging on to these. This isn't over." Phil rose and left her office. Immediately, Doloris picked up the phone and dialed.

"This is Doloris. We've got trouble…Phil Branson got his hands on the actual incident reports for Mrs. Solomon, Mrs. Cheavers, and Mrs. Ramsey…I don't know. That little twit must have made copies before she turned them in. No, you calm down…I'm not going to take the blame for this. If the police show up, I'm going to have to tell them the truth."

No sooner did Phil get back to his office, his cell phone rang.

"Phil, it's time we had a little heart-to-heart talk," Walter said.

Phil sipped a cup of coffee in the Whistle Stop Café, just down a few blocks from The Sanctuary, waiting for his table mate to arrive. Walter walked in a few minutes later. He waved to the waitress behind the counter.

"Hi, Martha." She waved back.

"Hello, Walter. Haven't seen you for a while." Walter pointed at Phil.

"I'll be over here. Bring over some coffee when you get a chance." She nodded. Walter helped himself down across from Phil.

"Well, you are a busy little beaver," Walter said. "I thought I told you to stay in your lane."

"I'm just cleaning up the mess you made."

"You're not paid to do that."

"I beg to differ. I've got family members who want answers. You think you can just sweep this under the rug? You're mistaken."

"It was all just an accident. Nobody meant for anyone to get hurt."

"Hurt? Mrs. Ramsey died. And it was completely avoidable, because you knew Wilfred Post was a loose cannon, but you did nothing. That makes us liable. And then you tried to cover it all up by destroying the evidence. That's a wrongful death lawsuit just waiting to flatten us."

"Well, I'm sure we can work something out with the family."

"Oh, I'm not done. The family is the least of your worries right now. Sylvia Longwood is dead. You remember her. She was the whistleblower. She had a kid, for Christ's sake. If I find out you had anything to do with her supposed drug overdose, you're going down." Phil rose to leave just as Martha brought over Walter's coffee. Phil smiled and pointed to Walter.

"He's paying." After Phil walked out the door, Walter got on his cell phone.

"It's me – Walter. We've got major problems. You better get control of Phil. If I go down for Sylvia, you're coming with me."

❖

Phil returned to The Sanctuary and slumped into his desk. Annie came in.

"You OK?" she said.

"What do I do now?" Phil said.

"Go to the police," Annie said.

"That's what's known as the nuclear option," Phil said.

"It's obvious what happened."

"Maybe. But there's what you know, and then there's what you can prove." Annie could not argue that. "I'm going to get some lunch and think about it. You know any nice quiet sandwich shops?" Annie gave it a moment's thought.

"Try Jake's Bar & Grill on 1st Avenue."

Phil sat in his booth at Jake's and mulled over his options. His cell phone rang.

"This is Phil."

"Phil, this is Darryl. How ya doin', buddy?"

"Why am I not surprised. You just been talking to Walter?"

"Yes, and I have to say, you are straying off the reservation. He is getting ready to serve you with a defamation lawsuit if you insist on going public with this wild claim that he had someone murdered. This company just can't support those sorts of irresponsible accusations."

"Darryl, these aren't wild accusations. We got a wrongful death here that was covered up, and the whistleblower just turned up dead."

"You just send me whatever evidence you have, and I'll have our legal department take a look at it. But you go public with any of this on your own, and you're going to hang yourself out to dry."

# CHAPTER 17

Phil knew he was drifting into uncharted waters. He dreaded the thought of crossing swords with his own company and the potential repercussions from any hasty accusations. He made copies of all the incident reports and security discs surrounding the Mrs. Ramsey case and over-nighted one set to Chicago for the legal department to peruse. The other set he kept just in case.

Let them deal with it, he thought. He kept Mrs. Ramsey's nightgown, since he could not make a copy of it. He felt that somehow this delicate piece of evidence might contain traces of DNA that could come in handy down the road.

Back in his office, he heard a light tap on the door.

"Come in," he said. Annie peeked her head in.

"Everything OK?" she asked.

"The monkey's off my back for now," Phil said. "I just dumped it all in the lap of the home office. Let them sort it out."

"Yeah, why not," Annie said. "In the meantime, I've got a little crisis that needs your delicate touch."

"Now what?"

"Mrs. Belvedere in 288 can't find her gold watch and claims it's been stolen," Annie said. Phil rolled his eyes.

"Get ahold of Fran and have her meet me up in Mrs. Belvedere's apartment." Lost items plagued every retirement community Phil managed. Most of the time residents simply misplaced them and blamed the staff for sticky fingers. One resident back in Orlando lost his hearing aids and swore they were stolen by nefarious housekeepers. Phil tried to reason with him that none of the housekeepers needed hearing aids and weren't stupid enough to try to sell them at a pawn shop. Nevertheless, the resident insisted they file a police report and fire his housekeeper. Before resorting to legal remedies, Phil insisted on conducting a top-to-bottom sweep of his unit. After an exhaustive search, the missing ear buds were finally located in his coat pocket hanging in the closet. Case closed.

Fran, the housekeeping director, rendezvoused with Phil, and together they knocked on Mrs. Belvedere's door.

"Well, it's about time you got here," Mrs. Belvedere said sharply.

"I understand you're missing a watch," Phil began.

"Not just any watch – it's gold plated with a wrist band that's probably worth thousands."

"Have you looked everywhere?" Fran asked.

"Of course, I have. It's obviously been stolen. My late husband gave it to me for our fiftieth anniversary. It's not just the money. It's a precious keepsake."

"Why don't we give the apartment another once over," Phil suggested.

"Why? What's the point? I always put it in its special box in my top dresser drawer. See –" she opened the dresser and displayed the empty jewelry box. "It's gone. Somebody stole it." Then she pointed at Fran. "One of your housekeepers, I'm sure. Or maybe one of the maintenance men."

"Let's just check your apartment one more time before we call the cops," Phil said. Mrs. Belvedere sat down in a huff as Phil and Fran turned the apartment upside down. They looked under the bed, inside shoes, under books, papers, magazines, inside the change bowl on her dresser. They stripped the bed, dug through the bathroom drawers, and checked every pocket in every garment in the closet. After an hour, they gave up.

"My son is a detective with the city of Billings. You need to call him to come over so I can file a theft report," Mrs. Belvedere said.

"Let me talk to my housekeepers first. Maybe they saw it and put it someplace for safe keeping."

"You go right ahead, but I'm calling my son." She picked up her phone and started dialing.

"Well, I can't stop you from calling your son. I'll talk to him when he gets here," Phil said. Fran excused herself and went in search of the housekeeper assigned to Mrs. Belvedere's unit.

In the early afternoon Sgt. Mike Belvedere arrived at The Sanctuary. He was in his late forties, salt and pepper hair, still fit from years on the force. Phil met him in the lobby. They talked as they walked to Mike's mother's apartment.

"I don't know what to say," Phil said. "We looked everywhere. Who knows where it is?"

"It's not the first time Mom has lost things. But I'll calm her down and touch base with the pawn shops to be on the lookout," Mike said.

Mike and Phil sat down on the couch in Mrs. Belvedere's living room as Mike filled out the report on his clipboard.

"It's just so upsetting," Mrs. Belvedere said. "That watch meant so much to me, and I've always taken such good care of it." She dabbed her eyes with a tissue at the thought of such a precious memory lost. When Mike finished the report, he stayed for a few minutes to chat with Phil.

"Can I get you an ice tea?" Mrs. Belvedere asked the two of them. She went to the refrigerator.

"Let me help you with the ice," Mike said as he rose to help. He turned to Phil. "It always gets stuck." Mike opened the freezer door and reached for the ice tray when he spotted the missing watch sitting on top of a box of frozen burritos. He lifted it out.

"Mom, look what I just found," he said as he turned in her direction. Mrs. Belvedere was speechless. She blanched with shame at the fuss she had made.

"Where was it?" she asked.

"In the freezer, where all expensive watches are kept," Mike said with a bit of irony. He handed the watch back to her and tore up the report he just completed.

"I can't even imagine why I did that," she said.

"Who knows, Mom. Just try to be more careful." He rose to leave and gave his mom a kiss on the cheek.

"Let me walk you out," Phil said. When they got to the ground floor, Phil angled Mike to his office.

"Are you in a hurry?"

"No – why?" Mike asked.

"I need some advice," Phil said. They retired to Phil's office.

"I'm not a policeman, so I don't know how this all works," Phil said. "So, if I tell you about a crime that I think might have been committed, can you just keep it to yourself until you've checked it out?"

"What kind of crime we talking about?" Mike said. Phil paused to consider the hornet's nest he was about to kick. From this point on there were no "take-backs", no "forget what I just said", or "never minds."

"Murder," Phil said. Mike raised his eyebrows.

"You think, but you don't know? Why? Is somebody missing?" Mike said.

"No. About a week ago the obits reported on a girl who died of a drug overdose – Sylvia Longwood. She used to work for us until about two months ago, when she quit and started working for Tip Top Home Health Care. Now, I know they do drug tests on new workers, so she couldn't have gotten hired if those tests came back positive. So, I seriously doubt she was a druggie."

"Why was her death ruled a drug overdose?"

"She was found dead in her car in the Rimrock Mall parking lot with a needle in her arm."

"What did the autopsy show?"

"I don't know – I don't have access. But her sister swears she wasn't using, and she had a kid she was raising on her own."

"OK. If that's true, who would want her dead?" Phil took a breath, but he knew the truth of the old saying – "In for a penny, in for a pound."

"She had information about a wrongful death at our facility that she was being pressured to cover up."

"Who?"

"Mrs. Ramsey."

"I remember that case. We did an investigation, and according to the incident report, it was just an unfortunate trip-and-fall."

"They didn't tell you the whole story," Phil said. He pulled out the three missing incident reports. "What you guys saw was doctored up. Sylvia made copies of these files before they got destroyed, and they tell a very different story." He handed the three incident reports to Mike.

"If the truth came out, the Ramsey family attorneys could hang us out to dry for negligence. We're talking millions of dollars."

"How did you get these?"

"Sylvia was the night nurse when Mrs. Ramsey fell. Her incident report was pretty incriminating. Somebody altered her report and forged her signature. I know personally that the security footage in front of the Ramsey apartment was doctored. I'm guessing she was pressured to lie to investigators. I went to see her a few days before she died, and she seemed really spooked and didn't want to talk to me. My theory is that somebody decided it was time to cover their tracks." He tapped the papers for emphasis. "What they didn't bank on was that Sylvia pulled these actual reports from the facility file before she quit and gave them to her sister for safe keeping."

"So, how did you get them?"

"Her sister gave them to me at the funeral. Apparently, Sylvia told her that if she died or went missing, to give these to me." Mike sighed.

"Jeez-louise," Mike muttered. "This thing's got a lot of moving parts."

"For starters, could you just snoop around and see if Sylvia's death seems fishy?"

"Yeah, sure," Mike said. "Give me a few days."

# CHAPTER 18

By the end of June Phil felt emotionally drained. He just finished haggling with Abbey, the food service director, over her excessive raw food budget for the last three months. She argued that everyone demands high quality meals, which contribute tremendously to overall resident satisfaction.

"No argument there," Phil agreed. "We rely on mealtime to be a major source of contentment. I know that if you deliver great meals three times a day, we'll be forgiven for almost any other failure. And for that we are grateful."

"Then stop riding me so hard about the budget," the food service director said.

"Fair enough. But I've been watching the kitchen crew taking leftovers home every single night," Phil said.

"Those are dishes that won't keep anyway – they spoil after a day. We either have to throw it away or let the kitchen crew take it home. So, what's the harm?"

"That's exactly the problem," Phil said. "That policy ensures the kitchen crew will cook enough of those perishable dishes to guarantee a mountain of leftovers at the end of every day."

"Not that much," Abbey said.

"I personally counted fifteen rotisserie chickens walk out the back door last Wednesday after dinner," Phil said. "We're not here to feed the staff – we're here to feed the residents. They are the ones paying for it. Starting next month I'm making a new policy – no leftovers go out the back door. Period. That should keep you under budget."

"A lot of my cooks don't get home in time to fix dinner for their family," Abbey said. "They rely on these leftovers to bring home a hot meal. It's a big morale boost you're taking away."

"Then let them pay for it, at our cost. That's a big discount."

"All right, I can live with that," Abbey nodded.

As residents filed into the dining room for dinner, Phil decided he needed a change of scenery. He grabbed his coat to head up-stairs, when he saw Annie clearing her desk for the weekend.

"You got any suggestions for a place I can grab a bite of dinner and get the flavor of this town?" Phil asked.

"I know just the place. The Wild Horse Saloon – downtown on 4th Street. Burgers, steaks, and ribs that'll spoil you forever. Only one thing – you'll need a partner."

"A partner? Why?"

"If you want the full monty, it's dinner and a two-step, and for that you need a partner."

"Sounds tempting. You offerin'?"

"Go get your cowboy on and meet me back down here in a half hour," Annie said with a grin. Phil summoned his reserves and donned his recently acquired cowboy accoutrements from Lou Taubert Ranch Outfitters. Looking like fresh rawhide, he stepped off the elevator and into the lobby, where he met Annie looking like a rodeo sweetheart.

"Well, ain't we a couple of dewdrops," Annie said.

The Wild Horse Saloon was the Billings hot spot since 2000, ground zero for western grub, dancing, drinks, and nightlife. By the time Phil pulled into the parking lot, couples in western gear angled their way to the front door like water through a fun-nel. George Strait's "All My Exes Live in Texas" resounded out the doorway and echoed into the night, beckoning all to the saloon's embrace. Phil found a two-seater near the dance floor, and they laid claim.

"We barely got here in time," Phil said. He stared out at the sea of cowboy hats bobbing up and down within this cavernous dining hall. To one side a frontier-style bar welcomed thirty cowpokes with its polished wooden bartop, brass boot rests, and bar stools shaped into saddles. In the center of the room a large dance floor offered ample space for a hundred high-steppers or more, all surrounded by a polished corral fence separating the diners from the boot stompers.

"It's Friday night, cowboy," Annie said. "This place is going to rock all night." A fetching college-aged waitress in tight jeans and boots handed the couple a menu.

"What are you drinking?" the waitress asked. Phil glanced at Annie for guidance.

"A couple of bottles of Coors," she said.

"Glad you spoke up – I was getting ready to order a merlot," Phil said. The waitress brought over two frosty bottles, as Phil examined the numerous trappings and wall hangings.

"I can't decide if this is a restaurant or a museum that serves food," Phil said.

"Both," Annie said. The walls displayed mounted cattle horns, framed chaps, lariats, a framed collection of 1800s-era barbed wire, branding irons, and classic black and white photos of cattle drives, rodeo riders in action, and dramatic wilderness scenery. Three-dimensional sculptures of mounted cowpokes stood on pedestals along the walls – a loving tribute to Frederick Remington.

Phil ordered the beef brisket and Annie chose the broiled chicken with fries. While the kitchen worked its magic, Phil and Annie got better acquainted.

"Tell me about Los Angeles," Phil said.

"That was just me trying to wash the Montana dust out of my hair."

"You were there for three years?"

"Yep."

"Doing what?"

"I divided my time between auditions, acting classes, and dance lessons."

"Did you land any parts?"

"I got a bit part in an episode of 'Grey's Anatomy.'"

"Wow, that's impressive."

"Yeah – it was a fifteen-second elevator scene. I stood behind Dr. McDreamy and Dr. Grey, with a couple of other extras in lab coats. When the doors opened and they walked out delivering their lines, the rest of us were just supposed to peel off to the left and right."

"That was it?"

"Yes, but I had my character's back story and motivation all worked out. They said I was very convincing as an elevator passenger."

"I see."

"I'd say in those three years I did 500 auditions, ten call-backs, and two gigs."

"So, why'd you leave?"

"Two years ago my mom fell and broke her hip, and I had to come back home here to look after her."

"What about your dad?"

"Heart attack took him five years ago. So, she needed me."

"Oh, I'm sorry to hear about your dad," Phil said. Annie searched her soul for her true feelings and knew her red carpet dreams were put on hold to play the real life role of a loving daughter. She teared up a bit.

"I'm ashamed to admit I felt some resentment that my mom stole my dreams. I knew if I went home I might never come back. Three years down the drain. I talked to my agent and he agreed that family comes first. So, I packed my bags and here I am."

"How's your mom doing?" Phil said. Annie wiped a tear away and smiled at life's twisted sense of humor.

"She passed away from complications three months after I got home." Phil sensed a twinge of bitterness in her voice.

"You did the right thing coming back. You'd have kicked yourself forever if you stayed in LA and missed those last three months."

"I know, I keep telling myself that. But god damn – never the luck."

"So, how did you end up at The Sanctuary?"

"I was looking for a place for mom to move into before she died. I stopped by The Sanctuary and found out there was a job opening for office manager. Seemed like a good fit, so I took it."

"Lucky for us. You happy here?"

"Yeah, I am. But I'll admit, I keep in touch with my agent."

"Fair enough. Everybody needs a Plan B," Phil said.

"My agent believes in me – he still calls once a month to see when I'm coming back. But I don't see it happening."

"Well, you never know. It ain't over 'till it's over," Phil said.

"Yep – you stole my line. So, what about you? How did you get to be such a super star?" Annie said.

"I just sort of fell into it – it was a good fit."

"How is it you're single – if that's not too personal?"

"I was married for about six months – Sherry was her name."

"What happened?"

"She died in a car accident. That was fifteen years ago. I was just never able to get back in the saddle."

"Hey – I'm sorry. I didn't mean to turn a perfectly good Friday night into a therapy session," Annie said.

"It's OK. You didn't know." The local cover band broke into the Allan Jackson classic "Livin' on Love."

"I love this song," Annie said. Phil paused to focus on the lyrics as the waitress delivered their dinner. Annie let the conversation lag, unsure of what topic to explore. They ate their meal in silence. In time, the announcer grabbed the microphone.

"OK, gents and gals, grab your partner and head to the dance floor for a little Texas Two-Step." Annie suddenly remembered the advice of her Los Angeles dance coach – "When in doubt, dance." She grabbed Phil by the hand.

"Let's join in," she said.

"I don't know any barn dances," Phil said.

"Don't be silly. It's the Texas Two-Step – slow, slow, quick, quick. That's all there is to it." She took him in her arms and demonstrated. About thirty couples formed a wide circle on the dance floor, side-by-side and arm-in-arm, poised for a counter-clockwise two-step shuffle to the beat of the music.

"You know what to do?" Annie asked. Phil grinned nervously.

"Sure – I've seen 'Urban Cowboy.'"

The band filled the hall with the strains of Hank Williams' "Hey Good Lookin'" and the entire circle of couples moved in unison to the musical rhythm of the slow-slow-quick-quick beat. Basic dancers just hung onto their partner and boot-stomped their way around the floor, while advanced couples strutted their stuff with turns, reverses, and other flourishes. But no matter the collective level of finesse on the dance floor, onlookers whistled and cheered the glorious sight of this dignified western promenade. Annie took the lead in gently showing Phil a few moves to add to their basic strut.

"Way to go – you look great," Annie said. "Are you sure you've never done this before?"

"I feel like I'm walking a tightrope," Phil said.

"Relax – you got more nerve than all these onlookers who just wish they had the guts to join in."

At the end of the song, Phil sighed with relief and led Annie off the dance floor. The announcer grabbed the microphone.

"And now we're goin' to give you all a chance to get romantic with a line dance waltz. So, grab your gal and git in line." Annie looked at Phil, hoping for a nod.

"We'll sit this one out, if that's OK," he said. Annie smiled agreeably and joined Phil back at their table. The dance floor filled with cowboys and their sweethearts in rows and columns, poised for the music to begin. The band played the delicate melody of Kenny Rogers' "Someone Feels Like a Fool Tonight" and the dance floor moved as one to the simple but elegant choreography of this well-known waltz routine. Phil sat mesmerized at the brotherhood of cowboys in motion. It seemed to him an utter incongruity to witness even the roughest bearded tough guys out there in front of God and everyone, lilting with graceful twirls and turns to this plaintive love song. The sight of it left him hypnotized. He could only compare it to the Asian notion of the harmony of yin and yang, go and jyu, masculine and feminine, strength and gentleness, all flowing together.

As the dance continued, Phil excused himself and strolled along the gallery where framed pictures told the history of rugged individualism out west. He paused at one compelling black-and-white of a Nebraska family in the 1800s, all posing for a photograph in the front yard of their humble sod dwelling. Sod, he thought – squares of mud bound together with an intricate web of earthen roots, stacked one on top of the other to form walls. The father, dressed in his Sunday best, sat proud in the front yard, shoulders back in a tall wooden chair, his woman by his side, surrounded by barefoot children. Phil locked eyes on this pioneer as he looked right back at Phil through the veil of time. The pride in the father's eyes amidst his meager possessions awakened Phil to an insight he had never considered.

At the end of the night as they walked back to their car, Phil shared his epiphany.

"I think I'm starting to get it," Phil said.

"Get what?"

"Back east we can't wait to see what's coming next – the newest gadget, the hottest trend. But out here folks seem to share a reverence for the way things used to be. Not everything, just the things that matter. I guess that's what you folks out here call the spirit of the west." Annie smiled.

"Yeah, you're gettin' it."

# CHAPTER 19

The next morning Phil got up early for a Saturday morning jog. He walked out of his apartment at 6:45 a.m. just in time to see Dexter Bailey quietly leaving Mildred Anderson's apartment down the hallway, with his coat over his arm. He lived in apartment 201, so he was definitely out of his neighborhood. Phil stopped short just out of curiosity. He knew Mrs. Anderson lost her husband five years earlier. He could not remember Dexter showing Mrs. Anderson any attention at mealtime or events, so this early morning departure bore all the trappings of the classic walk of shame. They both converged on the elevator landing at the same time.

"Good morning, Mr. Bailey," Phil said. "We're up early. Out for a walk?" Dexter just smiled as the elevator door opened. They both climbed aboard and Phil pushed the lobby button. Dexter breathed in the morning air deeply.

"Beautiful morning," Dexter said. Phil smiled back. Whatever went on in Mrs. Anderson's apartment was between two consenting adults, Phil reminded himself. No harm in a little senior romance. Who knows, it could blossom into something quite lovely, he mused. When the elevator door opened at lobby level, they both nodded and parted company.

Phil enjoyed his morning jogs. In June the sun rose around 5:30, and the temperature bottomed out in the mid-fifties, perfect for some outdoor exercise. His route took him behind the facility's swimming pool deck and into the woods behind the campus. A walking trail led through the trees to an open meadow, where deer often converged for breakfast. Flowers bloomed and the morning sky offered a shade of blue guaranteed to please. A half hour out and a half hour back, just what he needed to purge the body and soul of all toxins.

After a shower and a shave, he strolled through the lobby to greet any residents and staff that might pass by. Mrs. Cooper sat by the front door, waiting for her son to pick her up for breakfast, a routine that gave her great comfort.

"Good morning, Mrs. Cooper," Phil called out. She waved back and smiled. Phil's eye caught Tom Reese discreetly passing through the lobby on his way out the front door to a car idling under the porte cochere. Phil followed him out.

"Going somewhere?" Phil asked.

"Coffee," Tom said. "Care to join?"

"Actually, yes," Phil said. The two climbed into the burgundy four-door sedan. Phil turned to the driver.

"Morning, Dan," Phil said. "What's the occasion?" Without a word, Dan put the car in gear and the three got on the freeway and drove west about twenty miles to a truck stop just outside of Park City. As they drove, Dan broke the silence.

"Vincent, your son, Steve, he's being followed."

"What do you mean?" Tom said.

"Whenever he leaves town on business, he's got a tail."

"What about my daughter?"

"We haven't noticed any shadows with Jennifer, but we have to assume she's being tracked as well." Phil interrupted.

"Do you ever see your kids?" Phil asked.

"Twice in the last three years," Dan said.

"How do you manage that?"

"Secret messaging in the Billings classifieds," Dan said. "We arrange a meeting place that doesn't leave a paper trail – no airline tickets, no credit card receipts. Strictly cash."

"How do you notify each other of the time and place without drawing attention?" Phil asked. Dan pulled out an old classified ad from a file in the front seat and handed it to Phil.

"That's an ad we ran last year. Check out the 'For Sale' section." Phil opened the paper.

"What am I looking for?"

"Look for a rolltop desk for sale."

"OK – I found it. It says 'a lovely 1930 rolltop desk manufactured by Ideal Point'. The seller is asking $4,800. So?"

"Look at the manufacturer," Dan said. "It's always a two-word company. The two first letters of the first word are 'ID'. That's the postal abbreviation for Idaho. The first two letters of the second word are 'P-O'. That tells us the town will be Pocatello."

"How do you know when and where?" Phil asked.

"The date is found in the purchase price," Tom explained. "The second number is the month, and the first number is the day. '8' is August and the first number is '4' – August 4. We always meet across the street from the City Hall, and the time of day is found in the year the rolltop desk was manufactured – '1930'. In military time that's 7:30. We always meet in the evening, and spend one day together."

"Pretty clever," Phil said. He handed the classified ad back to Dan.

"So, how do you get there?"

"Dan picks me up and drops me off where the rental car will be waiting, rented to a prearranged identity. He gives me the matching rental agreement and driver's license, with enough cash for gas, lodging, and meals."

"And your son?"

"That's a little more tricky," Dan said. "We have to assume he's always under surveillance, so he has to do a little three-card-monte dodge to lose his tail, transfer to his travel car, and be on his way. He only uses cash for gas, lodging, and meals to avoid any paper trail."

"That's a pretty elaborate charade for one day with your boy," Phil said.

"We gotta make it look like he never left town," Dan said. "If these thugs think for one minute his kids know where he lives, they'll put a knife to his grandkids' throat to force them to talk."

"And this is how you expect to live for the rest of your life?" Phil said.

"What are my other options?" Tom said. Phil changed topics.

"How are you coming along with finding a new place for Tom – I mean Vincent?" Phil said.

"We're thinking about moving him to Guam. It's on the other side of the world, but it's still a U.S. territory, so he'll fit right in. The U.S. has a big Naval base there, a lot of military housing. We're building a back story right now so Vincent can blend in, play golf, go to the beach, start a new life."

"How soon?" Phil asked.

"A month or two."

Sipping coffee at the truck stop café, Phil sought more answers to quell his anxiety.

"I don't know about you guys, but I'm having trouble sleeping at night. Any day now a hitman could walk right through our front door without any warning."

"That's not going to happen," Dan said. "There is no trail that leads to your facility. Nobody knows Vincent's location except Walter Angler, me, and you."

"OK, that's easy to say, but for now let's just play 'what if.' Worst case scenario – for whatever reason – that dreaded hitman shows up. What am I supposed to do?" Phil said.

"In the first place, it's not going to be a surprise. You'll know when they're coming," Tom said. "I already worked this all out with your last administrator."

"Please clue me in," Phil said.

"If and when they ever make me, you'll get a call from a local number, or somebody in the appropriate uniform will walk right up to the front desk with a package, a basket of flowers, or a to-go order. They're going to ask for me by name and ask for my room number. That's how you'll know – 'cause nobody outside The Sanctuary should know my name or want to know my number. Nobody knows I live here, so nobody's mailing me anything, and I'm not phoning out for any pizza to go."

"OK, so somebody walks up to the front desk and wants to know where you live. What are we supposed to say?" Phil asked.

"You tell your receptionist to tell them that I'm in apartment 350."

"But we don't have a 350."

"They don't know that. They'll go up to the third floor and all the way to the end of the hallway before they figure it out. That will give us a couple of extra minutes to give me a heads-up to get out. That's why I live on the first floor."

"I don't like it. They'll be pissed. That's going to put all my people at risk," Phil said.

"No, they'll be pros. They're not going to go around shooting the place up."

"How many goons are we talking about?" Phil said.

"Two, probably three."

"OK, so what does my girl do after she tells them the wrong apartment number and then gives you the heads-up?" Phil said.

"She calls the police and then gets herself the hell out of there. I'll lay low out in the back woods until the cavalry arrives." Phil sighed and looked out the window disapprovingly. Tom saw the look on Phil's face. "I know it's the worst-case scenario, but that's our only play," Tom added.

"Once they know you're here, they'll just come back some other day. They'll find out where you live somehow, and because you live on the ground floor, they'll just come in through your window. None of us will ever see it coming," Phil said. He turned back to Dan. "You gotta get him out of here. I'm serious."

"I'm working on it," Dan said. Phil turned to Tom.

"No offense, but the sooner the better."

"I hear you," Tom said.

When they returned to Billings, Dan dropped off Tom and Phil at the front door and drove away.

"I'd like to show you something in my apartment, if you got a minute," Tom said.

"Sure," Phil said.

Tom lived in apartment 185, near the exit to the back patio. It was a modest and tidy apartment – dishes always washed and put away, clothes hung neatly, carpet spotless. A fully packed duffel bag with a Kimber 9mm semi-automatic pocket pistol in the side pouch sat by the front door, ready for a quick exit at any moment. Tom pointed to a painting hanging on his bedroom wall.

"I painted this myself – it's my wife." The portrait hung framed with loving detail, done in acrylics on a twenty by thirty-inch canvas. At the bottom he inscribed her name – "Leora." Her face rivaled the Mona Lisa for the subtle expression in her eyes and mouth, beckoning to the viewer to come hither.

"When did you do this?" Phil asked.

"I started it years ago – just finished it recently."

"She didn't sit for this?"

"Only briefly. She sat for me the night she died. Most of it I did from memory. I can close my eyes and see every little contour of her face, the turn of her eyebrow, the line of her chin, the gaze in her eye."

"It's amazing. The detail, the colors, that red in her dress."

"That blood red in her dress – that's her blood."

"You mean, actually?"

"Yes – actually." Phil decided to change the topic entirely.

"How did you learn to do this?" Phil asked.

"Painting has always been a hobby of mine. It's calming."

"Mister, this belongs in a gallery," Phil said.

"It's all I have left of her. She keeps me company and watches over me at night."

"I guess we both have something in common," Phil said.

"What's that?"

"We're both widowers. Yours died late in life, mine died six months after our wedding."

"I didn't know that," Tom said. "I'm sorry."

"Yeah – a damned car accident. I used to think that couples who lost a spouse late in life were the lucky ones. Guys like me that barely got off the launching pad. At least you had a lifetime of memories to comfort you. What have I got? Nothing but crushed dreams."

"I don't know," Tom said. "It's like, if you had to be blind, would you rather it be from birth or after a lifetime of sight? In the one case, you don't know what you're missing, but in the other case, you can count the cost of what you will never see again."

"Yeah, I get your point," Phil said. He turned to leave. "I understand you've been through a lot. I still need you out of here." Tom nodded in agreement.

Phil left Tom's apartment in search of Annie. She usually didn't come in on Saturdays, and after their late night at the Wild Horse Saloon he fully expected her to sleep in late. He rounded the hallway that emptied into the lobby and he spotted her at the reception desk, whispering and giggling with Tina. They both saw Phil approaching and conversation faded.

"Did I interrupt anything?" he said.

"Yes," Annie admitted freely. "We were talking about you."

"Uh huh," Phil said. He turned to Tina. "Can I borrow Annie for a few minutes?" Tina smiled.

"Take her for as long as you want. She's very distracting." Annie looked back at her and smiled. Phil did not seem amused.

"Let's go for a walk," Phil said.

"OK," Annie said. "Where to?" Phil said nothing, just headed for the front door. Annie followed, all the while wondering what might have prompted Phil's somber tone. Had she been overly insubordinate, she wondered? Once outside, Phil turned along the sidewalk that led around the building to the backyard and the swimming pool.

"You once asked me about the Tom Reese mystery," Phil began.

"Yeah?" Annie said.

"When I learned his little secret, I knew for sure that it was on a need-to-know basis – and at the time it didn't seem you needed to know. Understand?"

"Yeah. Sure."

"Well, the way things are going, I decided you do need to know."

"Why? Is he my long-lost half-brother?" They rounded the corner to find the pool area vacant. They chose a couple of loungers poolside and slid them closer together.

"What I'm about to tell you, you cannot repeat to anyone, not Tina, not your mother, not your priest. Understood?"

"Now you got me worried," Annie said.

"I mean it – even if you're alone in your own bathroom, don't even say it out loud to the mirror. Are we clear?"

"What the hell, Phil. OK." Phil paused and scanned the pool area – they were still alone.

"For starters, Tom Reese is not his real name," Phil said. Annie feigned a look of horror.

"No! I will definitely take that to the grave."

"Stop kidding around," Phil said. "His real name is Vincent Wallace. Three years ago he testified in a New York mob family case that put Santino Giovani in prison for life." Annie suddenly sobered up. "He went into the witness protection program, changed his name, got a little cosmetic work done, and has been hiding out here for the last three years trying to avoid detection."

"OK – so, why do I suddenly need to know?"

"That fellow who shows up here now and then and takes Tom for a couple days – he's the U.S. Marshal in charge of Tom's safety."

"Oh, my god, I had no idea," Annie said. "He's been living here all this time and I never had a clue. I mean, I knew he was a weird exception to some rule, with his empty file and all, but this is way out of left field."

"That's the idea. The problem is, there have been some developments that put this facility at risk, so they're making plans to move him somewhere else."

"Where?"

"That's not important. The important thing is that until he's gone we could be a target, so we need to have a plan ready."

"Ready for what?"

"There are people who want him dead."

"What are we supposed to do?"

For the next hour Phil explained the strategy cooked up by Tom and Walter Angler when he first moved in. He told her about the "Apartment 350" gambit and the absolute requirement of disappearing once the police were notified.

"Can Tina handle it?" Phil asked. "It'll all be on her."

"I'll see to it," Annie said.

"If we screw this up, people will die – you understand?" Phil said.

"Then, let's not screw it up," Annie said.

# CHAPTER 20

At the July 8 morning staff meeting, Phil shared the good news.

"I'm happy to report that our occupancy is at eighty-five percent. I want to thank everyone for your share in making this possible. Most of our move-ins come from word-of-mouth, and that doesn't happen without happy residents speaking well of us to friends and family. And you're the ones that keep them happy. So, pat yourselves on the back, and keep it up. But a special thanks goes to Susan Phillips, our marketing director. She's done a lot of hustling to fill this place. So, let's give her a hand." The room echoed with a genuine round of applause that put a blush on Susan's face.

After the meeting, Susan took Phil aside.

"First of all, thanks for the public pat on the back," she said. "Felt good."

"You earned it," Phil said.

"I've got a special request, if you don't mind," Susan continued.

"Sure. What's up?"

"Lyle and Vera Walters are celebrating their fiftieth wedding anniversary next week, and we thought it would be lovely if the facility could make that night special for them."

"What do you got in mind?" Phil asked.

"It's really a romantic story. They were at the International Hotel in Las Vegas in 1969 and had tickets to see Elvis Presley perform. He sang all the favorites. But when he sang his 1961 hit "Falling in

Love With You" Lyle was so moved by the moment, he proposed to Vera right on the spot, and they were married in Las Vegas that weekend. I was just wondering if we could somehow recreate that moment with a big party and an Elvis impersonator, or something like that."

"That is genius," Phil said. "And I know just the guy for the job."

"Really?" Susan said.

"Yes. His name is Sidney Howell. He's an Elvis impersonator down in Florida who's done this for years – entertains at all the retirement centers. I booked him for our Summer Fling program last year. Let me give him a call, see if we can fly him out."

"Oh, that would just be perfect," Susan said.

"Don't tell anyone until I get him booked," Phil said.

Sidney Howell was an aging Elvis impersonator. He never made the big time, but played in minor venues – rodeos, mall openings, corporate conventions – and lately found himself accepting any trivial gig. His agent signed him to perform at retirement communities for special "Elvis Night" programs for aging seniors. Residents just loved it, but he lamented the depths his professional life had sunk. However, he needed the money, so he reluctantly agreed to appear at these trifling events.

Phil still had his number on speed dial and gave him a call.

"Sid, this is Phil Branson. How ya doin', buddy?"

"Still above ground," Sidney said. "Thank you very much," he added in his Elvis twang.

"You busy these days?"

"Oh, you know, the usual convention stuff."

"I got a special request, if you'd consider it," Phil said.

"Whatcha got?"

"I'm running a retirement center out here in Montana these days, and we've got a couple celebrating their fiftieth wedding anniversary next week. I'd like to fly you out as a surprise to them and have you sing 'Falling in Love With You' as they renew their wedding vows. What do you say?"

"I don't know, Phil. That's a long way to go for just one song. Besides, I'm kinda done doing retirement centers. The crowds are too small and half of them fall asleep before the show is even over."

"You're going to want to do this one, trust me. Do this for me and I'll pay double your usual fee, plus all your travel expenses."

"I don't know," Sidney said. "This is really last minute. I'd have to juggle a lot of things around."

"Sid, if you ever needed a reminder that what you do makes a difference, this is the one," Phil said. Sid thought for a moment.

"What days are we talking?" Sid said.

The Walters' anniversary party took place in the facility's performance hall on July 20 at 5:00 p.m. Posters on the bulletin board announced the anniversary celebration and renewal of vows between Lyle and Vera Walters, with a special appearance of a mystery guest. The residents pressed Lester, the Activity Director, to reveal the identity of the secret guest, but he buttoned his lip. Phil refused to spoil the secret, and Annie remained hushed. On the day of the event the room resembled a Las Vegas banquet hall. Flashy posters of high-profile casinos, hotels, and marquee shows along the Strip hung on the walls, and famous recordings of Frank Sinatra, Wayne Newton, Dean Martin, and Tony Bennett echoed through the loud speakers and set the mood.

Streamers hung from the rafters, and a large mirror ball rotated in the middle of the room, sending flickers of light in all directions. Large round dining tables offered enough seating for 250 guests. Towers of mock poker chips served as table centerpieces, and decks of playing cards sat beside every place setting. Most residents arrived early to get a good seat, tickled at this stroll down memory lane. Many seniors swapped stories of money won and lost from their own trips to the Gambling Capital of the World.

At the designated moment a spotlight bathed the microphone front and center, and Phil Branson, in classic black suit and bowtie, welcomed everyone to this night of magic. A live band led the evening off with the classic song "Luck be a Lady Tonight" from the Broadway musical *Guys & Dolls*. Waiters delivered the dinner plates to each table, and the residents felt transported to an elegant feast worthy of The Bellagio.

After dinner and dessert, Phil stepped to the microphone to announce the special guest.

"Ladies and gentlemen, turn your eyes to the stage, put your hands together, and give a Las Vegas welcome to The Memphis Flash, the Tupelo Tornado, the King of Rock and Roll – Elvis Presley!" Phil stepped to the side, and with his finger pointing to the side curtain signaled Sidney Howell, a.k.a. Elvis Presley, to the stage. In all his bespangled excess, Elvis sprang into action, to the delight of the crowd. Many of the elderly residents were serious fans of the actual Elvis in his younger performing years, and the grey-haired widows turned absolutely giddy at the sight of this look-alike.

Sidney sang many of the Elvis standards – "You Ain't Nothing but a Hound Dog", "Love Me Tender", "Jailhouse Rock", "Don't Be Cruel", and "Suspicious Minds," delivering his signature imitation in words, song, and gyrations. Near the end of the show he turned to the audience for any "requests." That was Phil's cue to draw all eyes to the honored couple of the night. He stood, and the spotlight drew all eyes to him.

"Elvis, fifty years ago you performed a very special song at the International Hotel in Las Vegas that so moved a young couple in that audience with thoughts of love and romance, that the yearning bachelor proposed to his girl on the spot and she accepted his invitation 'till death do us part.' Through the magic of Las Vegas, that couple is here tonight, and if you would sing us that same song once again, they are prepared to renew their vows for another fifty years. Lyle and Vera Walters, will you please stand." The two lovers rose to their feet, and the auditorium fell silent.

"And now, Elvis, if you please," Phil said. With a portable mic in hand, Sidney stepped down from the stage and walked toward the happy couple, as the band played the opening strains of "Falling in Love with You." Sidney delivered that song with a new fervency and zest he had long since abandoned. The lights and music transported Lyle and Vera to that sacred night so many years ago, where they pledged their love forever and a day. Now, with tears in their eyes and hearts full, they renewed that solemn covenant and again sealed it with a kiss. "Elvis" continued his serenade while the celebrated couple slow-danced under the lights, joined by dozens of fellow seniors moved by the moment and the music. Phil stood in the shadows, glowing at this most tender display of devotion.

Annie quietly stepped up beside Phil.

"I know why I love this job. Now, I think I see why you love it so much too."

# CHAPTER 21

Residents could not stop talking about that night. For weeks, Phil received glowing words of appreciation for such a lovely night. Lester, the Activities Director, snapped a few candids of Lyle and Vera with Elvis and sent them to the *Billings Gazette*, which published them along with a touching article, regaling its readers with the night that Elvis came to town. Phil grabbed several copies of the paper off the newsstand and hand-delivered a copy to Lyle and Vera for their scrapbook. On his way back to the office, he again caught Dexter Bailey discreetly leaving the apartment of yet another widow. Their eyes met as they passed each other in the hallway, and Phil could swear Dexter gave him a sheepish grin. Back in his office, Phil called Annie in.

"I'm beginning to think we have a Casanova in the house," he said.

"What do you mean by that?" Annie said.

"I've seen Mr. Bailey leaving the apartment of two ladies in the past few weeks, one of them at 6:45 in the morning."

"Really?"

"And it seems whenever I see him, he's in the company of ladies – mealtime, activities, you name it."

"Men are in short supply here, so I wouldn't be surprised if his social calendar was always full," Annie said.

"I got no problem with honey bees visiting multiple flowers,"

Phil said. "I just need to make sure nobody's being exploited."

"Exploited? These are consenting adults, aren't they?"

"That's what I need to find out. The last facility I managed we had a Casanova who duped one lady out of $150,000 he promised to invest for her. He moved out a week later, and the police caught him at the airport bound for Europe. After wringing him out, they discovered he had sweet-talked four other widows out of a half million dollars."

"Oh, I see what you mean," Annie said.

"I think it's time I pay Mr. Bailey a visit," Phil said.

Dexter Bailey, in his fashionable leisure jacket, responded to the knock on his door to find Phil standing at his threshold.

"Why, Mr. Branson, what a pleasant surprise," Dexter said.

"I apologize for intruding without an invitation. Is this a bad time?"

"Actually, I am entertaining right now. Mrs. Willowby and I are sharing croissants. I am free this afternoon, however, if you care to stop by."

"Actually, you need to give Mrs. Willowby a rain check. You and I need to have a little talk."

"All right then. Please come in." Dexter opened the door wide and Phil helped himself inside. They walked to the living room, where Mrs. Willowby sat with a croissant and a mimosa.

"Good morning, Mrs. Willowby," Phil said. "I am so sorry to interrupt like this, but Mr. Bailey and I have some urgent business to discuss, and we are wondering if you might excuse us," Phil said. Mrs. Willowby looked at Dexter for confirmation.

"It's nothing, Elinor," Dexter said. "Let me stop by your place as soon as Mr. Branson and I are finished." He led her to the door, and with a kiss to the back of her hand, he sent her on her way.

"Now, what can I do for you, Mr. Branson?" Dexter said as they reconvened in the living room. Phil got right to the point.

"I can't help but notice how popular you are with the ladies." Dexter smiled in all modesty. Phil continued. "One thing I've told my golfing buddies is to just be patient – if they just live long enough they will be in very high demand."

"Yes, one of God's little jokes," Dexter said. "When it comes to the conquest of women, He makes it hard on us men when we are young and able, but oh so easy for us when we are old and worn out."

"That's why I'm here, actually. I have no objection to romance in one's twilight years, but one of my jobs here is to protect the vulnerable."

"Of course – perfectly understandable. And I would be disappointed if you didn't. So, let me put your mind at rest. I was in the women's clothing business for many years. When I retired I sold my company for $24 million. If you doubt me, I would be happy to instruct my accountant to share my bank statement with you. My wife and I expected to live out our golden years to the fullest. Sadly, she died of a heart attack six months later, and all of our plans died with her. For five years I wasted away in grief. My children pleaded with me to find comfort in the company of another woman, but the very thought seemed a violation of our covenant. However, one of my widower friends set me straight and explained the invaluable service we older men can provide for all these lonely women – good company, conversation, and the occasional warm bed. So I thought, well, I'd spent most of my life taking care of women's outside appearance. Maybe I might be able to attend to their inner needs now. So, I tried it and found out I was pretty good at it. My refrigerator is full of casserole dishes and confections from lonely widows looking for some affection, tenderness, and validation."

"Like, how many are we talking about?" Phil said.

"I would violate confidences if I divulged the names of all the ladies here who wait their turn for an evening with the likes of me. Let's just say it's a fulltime job. And each one I treat with dignity, and discretion. I have no need for their money, and wouldn't take it if it were offered. I consider this a very unique ministry that I have fallen into, that I am sure someone in your position should understand."

"I'm just still trying to catch up. Let me think about it for a while."

"Absolutely. Now, if you have no further need of me, Mrs. Willowby is waiting."

When Phil returned to his office, Annie popped her head in the door.

"How did it go? Is he a gigolo or just a con man?"

"Neither. I'd say for lack of a better word – I'd call him a therapist."

Sadly, two weeks later the front desk received a panicked phone call from Mrs. Pennington in 235.

"I need to speak to Mr. Branson," she said. The receptionist transferred the call.

"This is Phil Branson."

"Could you come up here right away – I think he's dead," she said.

"Who is dead?"

"Mr. Bailey."

A discreet visit to Mrs. Pennington's bedroom found Dexter nonresponsive. The police and EMT arrived at the same time to investigate the circumstances and rule out foul play. Sergeant Mike Belvedere was first on the scene.

"Considering your history here, I thought I'd better conduct a thorough inquiry this time to avoid another 'Mrs. Ramsey' snafu," Mike said.

"I'd appreciate that," Phil said. "And when you get a minute, I'd like to know how the Sylvia Longwood case is going."

"I'll get back to you. Let me do my work here first."

After all the evidence was collected, the coroner determined that Dexter simply died "in the saddle" as they say, much to the embarrassment of his bed partner, who apparently rode him a little too hard.

The funeral chapel swelled with heart-broken widows from The Sanctuary. Annie tried to do a head count, but gave up.

"This is amazing," Annie whispered to Phil at the close of the ceremony. "I've never seen such a funeral crowd for one of our residents. He must have made quite an impact."

"Let me put it this way – he was shared and passed around more times than a doobie at a Grateful Dead concert."

The company tasked with chiseling Dexter's headstone asked Phil for a fitting epitaph to engrave.

"I would borrow from Winston Churchill in his praise for the Royal Air Force in World War II – 'Never have so many owed so much to so few.'"

# CHAPTER 22

Annie rang Phil's office phone. "Sergeant Belvedere is here to see you." Phil checked his watch – 10:35 a.m.

"Did we have an appointment?"

"No," Annie said with a shrug.

"OK – send him in." Phil straightened up the clutter on his desk just as Mike and his partner, Earl Holick, stepped in. Earl stood a lean six feet, in his late thirties, with wispy brown hair.

"Is this a good time?" Mike said. Phil stood to shake hands. "This is my partner, Sergeant Earl Holick." Phil shook his hand as well.

"It's always a good time here at The Sanctuary," Phil said. "That's our motto."

"Catchy," Earl said with a grin.

"I thought you should know we are moving along with the Sylvia Longwood case," Mike said. "So, I thought we should give you a heads-up before we take it up a notch."

"Fill me in," Phil said.

"I can't go into every detail, but let me tell you what we can. We've interviewed Mrs. Solomon and Mrs. Cheavers and confirmed that Wilfred Post did in fact assault them in their apartment, and the facility covered it up. The videotape you gave us showed Wilfred entering and leaving Mrs. Ramsey's apartment on March 25. While he was in the apartment she fled into the hallway, where she

tripped and fell. That incident was not only scrubbed from the incident report, it was deleted from the footage of one of the security
cameras. That couldn't have been done by Sylvia Longwood."

"Of course not," Phil said. "Only Walter Angler had access to
the security footage." Earl had to correct him.

"Actually, Allan Dodge did too – head of Security. So, we can't
rule him out," Earl said.

"But here's something that got our attention with regard to
Sylvia," Mike continued. "The needle recovered from her arm was
manufactured by Monojet, which is the only brand used here at
The Sanctuary. But at the time of her death she worked for Tip Top
Home Care, which only carries BD syringes – Becton/Dickinson.
So, it seems odd that she would be using a needle from The Sanctuary, where she hadn't worked for over a month. It would be more
likely, and easier, for her to lay her hands on a needle from her
current employer's inventory."

"Yeah, good thought," Phil said.

"Now, this is all circumstantial and doesn't prove anything. But
it does cast doubt on the drug overdose theory," Mike said.

"And we've interviewed Sylvia's sister and co-workers from Tip
Top," Earl said. "And nobody thinks she was a drug addict. If she
was, somebody would have noticed. You just can't hide that life-
style from everybody."

"So, what do you think happened?" Phil asked them both.

"In light of the other cover-ups, we suspect higher-ups here,
who certainly had motive and opportunity," Mike said.

"Have you got enough to arrest anyone?"

"No, not enough evidence to arrest, but certainly enough to
question some people, starting with Doloris Chastain, the Personal
Care Director here," Mike said.

"Is she in today?" Earl asked.

"Yes."

"We need to interview her," Mike said. "But we don't want to
make a big scene or get all the busy-bodies in the building worked

up. We could ask her to come down to the station, but if you have a private room somewhere, we could talk there."

"You can have my office. I can call her down and the two of you can talk to her here. Would that work?"

"That would be fine, if you don't mind," Mike said. Phil picked up the phone and dialed the Personal Care desk.

"This is Phil – is Doloris in?...OK, I'll hold." Phil gave Mike a nod. "Yes, Doloris, this is Phil. Could you come down here to my office for a few minutes?...No, it won't take long...OK, thanks." Phil hung up the receiver and turned to Mike.

"She's on her way. You think she's involved?"

"Not sure," said Earl.

"We're going to ask her some questions – see what she says. If she clams up, I'm going to have to rattle her cage a little and see how she reacts. If she was just taking orders for someone else, she's not going to want to take the fall for murder."

"You think she'll squeal?" Phil said.

"Probably not," Mike said. "But I wouldn't want to be the first person she calls after we're done with her."

"Why? Who do you think she'll call?"

"Hard to tell," Earl said. "But we've got Walter Angler's home phone bugged right now and a $5.00 wager between Mike and me."

Doloris walked off the elevator in her blue scrubs and made her way to the executive office suites. She spotted Phil standing outside his office and nodded politely as she approached.

"Morning, Doloris," Phil said. He opened his door and waved her in, then closed the door behind her.

Inside, she saw Sgt. Mike Belvedere, leaning back on Phil's desk, and Earl Holick leaning against the far wall. By the look on their faces she knew this was no social visit.

"Mike, what a surprise," she said.

"Hello, Ms. Chastain. This is my partner Sergeant Holick. I hope you don't mind if we skip over the pleasantries. We're here on official business." A sudden wave of anxiety washed over her.

She fiddled with her name tag and nervously searched for the top button of her tunic, which had no buttons. Mike took charge of the interview as Earl watched.

"We need to ask you a few questions, if that's all right," Mike began.

"About what?" Doloris asked.

"About the Mrs. Ramsey incident a few months back."

"What about it?"

"Oh, just a few details we need to clear up. We thought maybe you could help."

"I thought this whole matter was resolved a long time ago."

"There was really no need for a deep dive investigation for a simple trip-and-fall, but once Mrs. Ramsey died, the family insisted on a thorough probe to rule out any possible negligence."

"Well, it's all in the incident report," Doloris said. Mike opened a file and lifted out a sheet of paper.

"You mean this one?" Doloris looked at the report and nodded.

"Yes, that's the report. So, what's your question?" Mike then lifted out the original report filled out by Sylvia and handed it to Doloris.

"Can you explain to me why this report is different?" Doloris nervously scanned the original report, which detailed the Wilfred Post invasion.

"Where did you get this?" Doloris said.

"Notice the signatures at the bottom," Mike pointed out. "They both say 'Sylvia Longwood,' but the signatures are not the same. Can you explain any of this?"

"No."

"We had a handwriting expert verify that this was Sylvia's signature," Mike said, pointing to the one page. "The other is a forgery. That makes this report invalid, and the other report legit," Mike said, as he laid down the forgery and held up the true report. "Now, forging an incident report is a serious offense, wouldn't you say?"

Doloris just stared at the wall. "Doloris?" Mike said with more insistence.

"You could get fired, maybe lose your license. This is your department, isn't it? How do you explain all of this?" Doloris sat in silence, dying a thousand deaths.

"Can you tell me why Sylvia Longwood quit working for The Sanctuary the very next day?"

"No."

"Really? You have no idea?" Mike said.

"She just called the next day and said she quit."

"Did you ask her why?"

"No."

"Are you aware she died about a month ago?"

"Yes, I heard about it."

"It was ruled a drug overdose. Now, we checked with Tip Top Home Care – they drug screen all their applicants, and Sylvia came up clean before she was hired. So, she wasn't a druggie. But then a month later she OD's. That make any sense to you?"

"I don't know. I guess anything can happen," Doloris said.

"Funny thing is, she had a Monojet syringe needle stuck in her arm when they found her body. Same brand of needles you stock here – correct?"

"Yes."

"You know what kind of needles they stock at Tip Top Home Care?"

"No."

"BD – Becton/Dickinson. So that needle in her arm – it didn't come from her place of business. So, any idea how she could have gotten one of your needles?"

"We're not the only facility that uses Monojets."

"Oh – you think it would have been easier for her to just sneak into a facility she didn't work for and grab some needles from medical storage while nobody's looking?"

"You can buy Monojets online. It's no big deal," Doloris said.

"Maybe so. You think that's what she did? Because Sylvia's sister gave us all of Sylvia's credit card receipts for the last six months, and there's no Monojet purchases."

"I think if you don't have any other questions, I need to get back to work."

"I guess we're done. But I'll tell you one thing. I don't think she overdosed. I think she was murdered. Don't you? You wouldn't know anything about that, now would you?"

"I've told you everything I know. If you need anything else, you can talk to my lawyer," Doloris said with as much bravado as she could fake. Without asking permission, she rose to her feet and saw herself out.

# CHAPTER 23

Doloris did not go back to her office, but instead walked straight out the front door, to her car, and drove away from the facility. She felt her heart pounding and her hands trembling as she drove. She pulled off into a supermarket parking lot to compose herself. After several minutes, she reached into her purse for her cell phone.

"Hello, this is Walter."

"You're not going to believe who I've just been talking to," Doloris said.

"Who?"

"The police. They had me down in Phil's office asking questions about the Ramsey incident reports and Sylvia."

"Where are you?"

"I'm in the parking lot of Albertson's."

"Well, what did you say?"

"What could I say? Phil must have given them the actual original incident reports. They showed them to me and pointed out the forgery. Did you actually think your fake signature would hold up? They spotted it right away."

"Just calm down. They don't have anything," Walter said.

"What do you mean, they don't have anything? They have everything, and it's my neck in the noose."

"Well, if you'd been more careful watching Wilfred Post, none of this would have happened. This is all your fault," Walter said.

"I'm not the one who stuck the needle in her arm, and I'm not going to jail for you, you can be sure of that."

"Maybe not instead of me, but you're coming with me – it's called conspiracy. So, you just better get it together and shut your mouth." Doloris hung up the phone and sat in the parking lot, trying to imagine any scenario where she walked free. She envisioned the shame of a public trial, the humiliation of her family, the scorn of her friends, the loss of everything she cared about. She gave up and drove home. In her bathroom medicine cabinet she lifted out a bottle of prescription sleeping pills, filled a glass of water, and locked her bedroom door.

Back at the station Mike and Earl listened to the recorded phone call between Walter and Doloris. Mike turned to Earl.

"That seals it. Time to pay Walter a visit."

"You owe me five bucks," Earl said.

The two drove out to Walter's house and rang the doorbell. Walter's wife opened the door.

"I'm Sergeant Belvedere and this is Sergeant Holick, with the Billings Police. Is your husband home?"

"No, he left about a half hour ago," Clara said. "Is anything wrong?"

"Do you know where he went?" Mike asked.

"He just said he had some business to attend to."

"What kind of car does he drive?" Mike said.

"He drives a Lincoln Continental, dark blue," she said as she nervously clutched her blouse. Earl handed her his business card.

"If you see him, would you please have him give us a call," Earl said.

"I don't understand. Is he in trouble?" she asked.

"Just have him call us," Mike said. As they walked away Mike gave the garage a look. The garage door was open and the stall was empty.

"What do you think?" Earl asked.

"He knows the jig's up. I hope he's not stupid," Mike said.

"Shall we put a BOLO out?" Earl said. Mike sighed.

"Yeah."

Walter knew he had only one card to play to save his neck. He went to the bank where his safety deposit box held a pen voice recorder containing a sensitive conversation between himself and his boss, Darryl Brooks, Director of Operations for United Senior Living. He removed the pen from the box and placed it in his coat pocket, then left the bank. Once in his car he made a call from his cell phone.

"United Senior Living," the receptionist said.

"This is Walter Angler calling for Darryl Brooks."

"I'll put you through," she said, and placed him on hold.

"There is a Walter Angler on line two," she said to Darryl on his private line.

"Thanks. I'll get it." Darryl punched line two. "Walter, what's up?"

"I've got a recording you need to hear. Just listen to this," Walter said, then pushed the PLAY button on his pen recorder and put it next to the receiver. Although the voice quality was a bit grainy, the voices of Walter and Darryl could not be mistaken.

> *What do you think?*
> *I don't like it. She could put us all in jail.*
> *What do we do?*
> *We have to make sure she doesn't talk. Ever.*

Walter pushed the STOP button.

"You recall that conversation?" Walter said.

"What the hell have you done?" Darryl said.

"The police are probably looking for me right now to find out what I know about Sylvia Longwood's death."

"You think you're going to pin it on me? I never touched that girl."

"You gave the order, and I've got the recording to prove it. A little insurance policy. That's conspiracy to commit murder. So, don't
think for one second you're home free."

"OK, so why'd you call?"

"Just to let you know, first of all, if I go down, you're coming
with me."

"Look, I'll get you the best attorney money can buy. If you were
careful, they've got no physical evidence to connect you with her
death. It'll never go to trial. And when you walk, there'll be a million dollars in a trust account in your name. But you gotta destroy
that recording."

"I'll tell you what – you hand-deliver a cashier's check for a half
million up front, and I'll consider it a good faith gesture. Otherwise
you may want to disappear. We clear?"

"It'll take me the better part of today to pull that much cash
together. I'll fly out tomorrow."

Walter returned home to see a police car already in his driveway. He got out of the car and braced himself for the ordeal ahead.
Sergeants Belvedere and Holick opened the front door and met
him in the front yard.

"We need to bring you to the station for questioning," Mike
said.

"Am I being charged with anything?" Walter asked.

"Not yet."

"Clara –" Walter called to his wife, who stood on the front
porch. "Have our attorney meet me at the station."

"All right, dear. Is everything OK?" she asked.

"Yes, everything's fine. It'll all get sorted out." Mike and Earl
escorted Walter to the squad car, and the three pulled out of the
driveway. At the station Earl sat Walter in an interview room to
wait. In a few minutes Mike and Earl entered with a laptop computer.

"Are you thirsty? Can we get you anything?" Mike asked.

"No, I'm fine."

"Mind if we get started?" Mike said.

"I'd like to know what this is all about," Walter said.

"Did you know a girl by the name of Sylvia Longwood?" Mike asked.

"Sure. She worked for us at The Sanctuary."

"Did you know she turned up dead about a month ago?"

"I read about it in the paper – something about an overdose."

"Yeah, they found her in the Rimrock Mall parking lot," Mike said.

"OK, so what does that have to do with me?" Walter said.

"Do you recall where you were on the evening of June 17?" Mike asked.

"Not right off. I'd have to think about it." Walter said. Mike opened the laptop and turned the screen to Walter.

"They've installed surveillance cameras around the Rimrock Mall parking lot, on the tops of certain light poles, you know, just to keep an eye on things. We studied the footage from June 17 – that was the day that Sylvia was found dead. Take a look at the top of the screen – it's time stamped. It's the closest camera to where she was parked, so we had to enlarge the picture." Walter nervously looked at the footage. He hadn't thought about security cameras. Suddenly it was clear to him why Sylvia chose the mall parking lot to meet. Mike pointed to the screen.

"See, there's her Civic pulling in and parking. Now, let me fast forward about fifteen minutes." He pushed a button to advance the film. "OK – now, looky here – isn't that your Lincoln Continental pulling up beside her?" Walter began to feel drops of sweat trickle down his back. "Now, isn't that you getting out of your car and getting into the passenger seat of her Civic?" Before Walter could think of what to say, Richard Carlton, Walter's attorney, entered the room.

"Are you questioning my client without the benefit of counsel?" Richard said.

"They were just…" Walter started to say.

"Walter, don't say another word." He turned to Mike. "Sergeant, have you read Walter his rights?"

"We haven't charged him with anything, just asking some questions," Mike said.

"We're done here," Richard said.

"Now wait," Mike said.

"No – if you haven't charged him with anything, he doesn't have to answer any questions." He turned to Walter. "C'mon, let's go." As Richard ushered his client out, Mike called out.

"Don't leave town."

# CHAPTER 24

The next afternoon Walter got a call.

"I'm here in town. Where can we meet?" Darryl said.

"You're not at the airport?"

"No – I decided to drive."

Walter did not like the sound of that. If Darryl drove all the way from Chicago, rather than fly, that was an eighteen-hour ordeal, and he would only do that for one reason – to avoid leaving a paper trail that could place him in Billings. And there was only one reason for that. Just as a precaution, he set up the meeting place where cameras would record the event.

"Sure. Let's meet at the Rimrock Mall parking lot north side. I'll be in a blue Lincoln Continental. Let's say 5:00 p.m." Before leaving the house, Walter wrapped his incriminating recording pen in a small box and took it to the post office. He addressed it to his wife with a message inside – "Please give this box to Sgt. Belvedere." If he survived his meeting with Darryl, he could retrieve the box when it arrived in the mail. Otherwise, his widow could make sure his murderer got his comeuppance.

"I've got to meet somebody in town. I'll be right back," Walter said to his wife. He drove to the north side parking lot and looked for a spot close to one of the surveillance cameras placed high overhead. At 5:00 p.m. Darryl's Pontiac Grand Prix with Illinois license plates rolled up alongside Walter's Lincoln Continental. He waved

Walter over to join him in his car. Walter obliged, confident the "eye in the sky" would capture everything on film. He even glanced up at the camera briefly to be sure it recorded his face. The Grand Prix sat in its spot for about two minutes, when the camera captured the flicker of muzzle flash twice reflecting off the dashboard windshield. Then the Pontiac slowly drove away with its two occupants, leaving the Lincoln Continental behind.

When Walter never returned home, Clara became worried. By 11:00 p.m. she called a few friends he might have shared a drink with. Nobody had seen him. She widened the search to include The Sanctuary, but her call simply went to the answering service. She called their attorney, Richard Carlton, but he could not imagine where Walter might be. Finally, she called Sgt. Mike Belvedere, dialing the number on the business card he'd given her.

"I'm sorry, Mrs. Angler, I have no idea where he might be. He left the police station with his attorney yesterday and that's the last I've seen of him. I hope he hasn't left town."

Darryl knew he had to dispose of the body, and any old remote section along Highway 12 seemed as good as any. After about five hours of driving, he got sick of looking at the blanketed body of Walter and searched for a wide open remote section of the highway to dump the body. About ten miles east of White Butte, South Dakota, he pulled off on the shoulder. He got out and walked down the embankment, which dropped off slightly to a small creek.

Perfect, he thought. I'll just dump the body in this creek. Nobody can even see it from the road. The coyotes will have it for dinner before anyone is any the wiser. He climbed back up to the car and opened the passenger door. Walter's limp body dropped out. He caught it and reached under his arms to hoist him out. Just as he began to pull, a lone motorist pulled up to a stop behind him, opened his door, and stepped out.

"Car trouble?" the motorist called out.

"No, just stretching my legs," Darryl said. The motorist suddenly realized he should stretch his own legs. He walked toward Darryl. Slightly panicked, Darryl shoved Walter back into the car and tried to close the door, but with Walter leaning against it, he struggled as the good Samaritan approached. Finally, with a desperate thrust, he pushed the door closed and leaned against it.

"I drive this stretch every few weeks, and I'll admit it wears me out," the motorist said. Darryl remained on the passenger side of the car as the motorist closed in on the driver's side.

"You can drive this highway and not see another car for miles. That's why I thought I'd stop and make sure you weren't stuck." He glanced in the driver's side window and saw a big lump wrapped in a blanket. Too big for a dead animal, and sure enough it could be a body, he thought. That, combined with Darryl's slightly anxious mannerisms, told him to move on.

"Well, I'll leave you to it," the motorist said. "Where you headed?"

"Minneapolis," Darryl said. The motorist nodded.

"Good luck to you," the motorist said. He got back in his car and jotted down the license plate of the Pontiac, and noted the mile marker, then started up his engine and drove on. Once out of sight, Darryl quickly opened the passenger door again and dragged Walter to the edge of the embankment and down to the creek. He quickly checked Walter's pockets to rid him of any identification, then climbed back up the shallow slope, climbed into his car, and motored east.

The phone rang at the Lemmon, South Dakota, Police Department.

"Lemmon Police," the officer said.

"Yeah, this is Harold Graham. I was just driving east on U.S. 12, about five miles west of Lemmon, and I came across a car off on the southside shoulder, just east of Township Road. It looked like the driver was trying to dump a big heavy object down in the creek."

"Could you tell what it was?" the officer said.

"I couldn't tell for sure, and I didn't want to stick around to find out," Harold said. "I just thought somebody might want to take a drive out there and take a look."

"Did you get the license number?"

"Yeah." He rattled off the plate numbers.

"OK, thanks for the heads-up. I'll have one of our guys take a drive out there."

❖

Phil came to work the next morning to be met by Annie with dreadful news – Doloris Chastain's daughter found her dead in her bedroom from an overdose of sleeping pills, and Walter Angler was missing.

"What am I going to do now?" he said. There was no doubt in his mind that Doloris spiraled into despair from Mike's piercing line of questioning. As for Walter, Phil could only suppose Walter foolishly made a run for it and would soon be apprehended. Two days later the mailman delivered a small package to the Angler home. Clara retrieved it from the mailbox and took it inside. Her curiosity prompted her to open the wrapping and lift the lid to see an oversized pen. In her haste to open the box, she gave no notice to the tightly folded message tucked in the inside of the box lid. It looked like part of the wrapping to keep the pen from jiggling. She studied the pen in one hand as she tossed the box with the message into the trash.

What a funny gift, she thought. I wonder who it's from? She examined the pen briefly, then left it on the desk in the den.

The mall's parking lot security officer noticed that Walter's car sat unmoved for two days. He flagged the car with a notice tucked under the windshield wiper to move the vehicle within twenty-four hours or incur a towing fee. When the car's owner did not respond, a local tow truck hauled the vehicle to the city impound. The impound secretary made a search of the registered owner from the license plate and called the Angler residence.

"Is Walter or Clara Angler there?" she said.

"This is Clara Angler."

"This is the Billings City Impound. We have your Lincoln Continental here, and you need to come pick it up."

"It's at the impound? How did it get there?" Clara asked.

"It was towed here yesterday. Just so you know, there is a towing fee of $150 plus $35 a day for every day it sits on our lot."

"Oh, dear. I'll come right over and get it." She grabbed a set of spare keys and called a friend of hers to drive her over. At the impound she apologized for the inconvenience.

"I don't know why my husband abandoned the car. It's not like him. Where was it?" The secretary checked the impound slip.

"It was at the Rimrock Mall."

"Well, that's odd," she said. "How much do I owe you?"

"A hundred fifty for the towing fee plus four days' storage – that comes to $290." Clara wrote out a check, apologized again, then drove the Lincoln home and put it in the garage, still hoping Walter would eventually show up with a good explanation.

A week later at Doloris' funeral service, Phil stood near the back of the graveside assembly, where he spotted Mike Belvedere.

"I feel terrible about all this. I didn't think we leaned on her that hard. The review board investigated and cleared us, but this," he pointed to the funeral, "I can't explain it."

"What about Walter? Whatever happened to him?" Phil asked.

"Still missing. We've flagged all his credit cards, so the next time he uses them we'll nail him." Phil suddenly felt the need to notify the home office. He slipped away from the crowd to get back to work.

"United Senior Living," the receptionist said to the incoming call.

"This is Phil Branson. I need to speak to Darryl Brooks."

"Hold the line," she said. In a moment Darryl picked up.

"Phil, how's the world treating you?"

"Well, I got good news and bad news. Which do you want to hear first?"

"Let's start with the good news."

"We're closing in on ninety percent occupancy – should be there by the end of the month."

"Fantastic. I knew you could turn things around."

"Wait till you hear the bad news. That wrongful death situation we talked about before – the police have gotten involved. Our Personal Care Director took her own life over her involvement in the cover-up, and Walter Angler has gone missing."

"This is unbelievable. What have you done? I told you to let our legal department handle it."

"If the legal department had actually handled it, we wouldn't be having this conversation," Phil said.

"You've exposed us to so much liability, you have no idea. The press is going to kill that facility, and the lawsuits will bury this company."

"If you'll just get out in front of this thing, nobody's going to blame the company. These are the actions of a few misguided people. One of them is dead and the other is missing. I'll clean this mess up as much as I can from my side. It'll take some time to heal, but we've got to start generating some positive PR to win in the court of public opinion."

"How do you propose we do that?" Darryl said.

"Remember that big senior festival we held last year at the Terracina Grand?"

"Yeah – I remember it cost a fortune."

"You're looking at it the wrong way. Ask yourself what it's worth to have the governor come visit us. Ask what all that free publicity is going to do for The Sanctuary – what your cash flow is going to be when you're full with a waiting list," Phil said.

"How much is it going to cost?"

"I'll need an advance of $100,000."

"A hundred thousand?"

"We're going to put on an antique car rally, senior fashion show, golf tournament, arts and crafts competition, live entertainment. We'll schedule it right on the heels of the Montana Fair in early September, when everybody's still in town from across the state."

"Can you get it all together in just six weeks?"

"Just watch me."

"All right. I'll have accounting wire you the money."

"You won't be sorry."

"Don't let me down."

"Oh, by the way, has Walter gotten in touch with you for any reason?"

"No. If he helped create that mess out there, he's not going to get any sympathy from me."

# CHAPTER 25

In late July Marion Federal Prison transferred an ailing Santino Giovani to the St. Louis University Hospital to evaluate and treat his recently discovered stage four lung cancer. For the past year he complained of fatigue, coughing, and difficulty in breathing, but refused any medical interventions that might interrupt his lifelong cigarette habit. While smoking was banned in prison, inmates with Giovani's clout managed to maintain their addiction. But when he started spitting up blood, prison doctors had no choice. The CT scan revealed cancer spots in his spine, lungs, and brain. Doctors gave him only weeks to live. Lying in his hospital bed, he faded in and out of his medicated state.

His two sons, Johnny and Marco, sat by his side for any comfort they might offer and instructions they might receive. He long since lost interest in eating – feeding tubes provided sustaining fluids. Three days earlier Santino exhausted himself enumerating all unfinished business for his boys to resolve. With his vital forces fading, he opened his eyes to deliver his final demands – which fell under the heading "Scores to Settle." He reached out to grasp Johnny's hand, as if to transmit his words viscerally. With labored breathing, he gently drew Johnny close.

"C'mere," Santino said. Johnny inched closer to his dying father.

"I'm done. I got no fight left," he muttered. "I saved this request to the last." He paused to inhale. "I need to know that you will never rest until you find the man who put me here. You gotta swear on your sainted mother's grave that you will take his life the way he took mine, with no mercy." Then he squeezed his son's hand with his last ebbing ounce of verve. "Swear it – both of you." Johnny and Marco clenched their teeth with renewed dedication.

"We swear, Pop," they said. "We swear we will hunt him down and personally bury him."

Santino Giovani was laid to rest the following Saturday as throngs of onlookers lined the streets to catch a glimpse of the larger-than-life funeral procession carrying the legendary convicted mob boss. He was mourned in a private service and taken to a cemetery where he might spend eternity with fellow mobsters who had long since ceased caring about the company they kept. His two sons stood graveside with family and associates to pledge their lives and fortunes in preserving his pernicious legacy.

Mr. Diamond accepted Johnny's request for an update on his efforts to locate Vincent Wallace. In his New York City warehouse office, Johnny welcomed the infamous manhunter to his conference table.

"In case you didn't know, my father passed away last week," Johnny said.

"Hard to miss with all the media coverage. You'd have thought he was Gandhi," Mr. Diamond said.

"He was the aggrieved party that prompted this manhunt, so I just wanted to reassure you that his death in no way diminishes our interest in finding Vincent Wallace. If anything, it intensifies our determination to unearth this rodent."

"Understood," Mr. Diamond said. "I assume you're running the show now."

"That's right. And tying up this loose end is of critical importance if I expect to be taken seriously by subordinates and competitors. Now, you've been at it for four months now. I'd like a progress report, if you don't mind," Johnny said.

"Certainly. The first thing we did was to test the Marshal Service for leaks. Somebody knows where he is – we just don't know who. We hoped we might get lucky if we splashed some money around. We pressed all of our contacts as hard as we could, with no success. That just meant we were going to have to do this the old-fashioned way. We have his two kids under surveillance, and we have their credit cards flagged for any unusual airline travel or out-of-state gas receipts. We've hacked into the phone company to get access to their phone records, with special interest in long distance calls. So far, no cigar. That just means that they're probably using burner phones to stay in touch."

"If you think his kids know where he is, why don't you just squeeze the information out of them?"

"I run a legit business and I make good money at it. I can't afford to torture and whack people the way you do. That's what put your father in prison. If you want this guy that bad, go beat up his kids yourself. Besides, I don't need to get heavy-handed. Sooner or later they'll get lazy. The son made a trip to Seattle last month. I followed him. But it turned out to be just a business trip."

"Any out-of-town visitors?" Johnny asked.

"We mounted a security camera high up on the telephone pole across the street from the homes of both his kids. We watch everyone who comes and goes."

"What about the internet?"

"We're hacked into the e-mail accounts of both kids. We read everything, and we track down the source of every e-mail sender."

"Anything else?"

"I have a bank of computers that are programmed to do nothing except read every city newspaper in the country and flag certain key words that our subject might use, like the names of his kids, grandkids, his wife, close relatives, any schools they attended, or companies they ever worked for."

"OK," Johnny said.

"Trust me, somebody's going to make a mistake. It always happens," Mr. Diamond said.

"You said the longest job took you eight months?" Johnny said.

"Yes."

"You're halfway there."

"This job's not going to take that long. I got a feeling about this," Mr. Diamond said. Johnny nodded.

"All right, then. Just do it," Johnny said.

Over the weekend Phil met with Annie at the Wild Horse Saloon for lunch and a preview of the Fall Festival he planned to rehabilitate the name and reputation of The Sanctuary.

"This sounds like a job for Superman," Annie said. "If you can pull this off, it'll be a huge win for everyone – the staff, the residents, and the families, who right now are all a little bit worried about how shaky things are looking. I mean, just think about it – in the last month we've seen a resident and ex-employee die, a department head commit suicide, and the previous administrator disappear. It's not looking good."

"I know. I really bit off more than I could chew when I took the reins here," Phil said. The waitress brought over his hamburger platter and Annie's Cobb salad.

"Eat your lunch," Annie said. "I got a good feeling about you. If anybody can save this sinking ship, you can."

At the Monday morning staff meeting Phil had plenty to say.

"First, I want to express my sadness at the passing of Doloris Chastain. We've hired a new Personal Care Director that I know you are going to like," he said, pointing to the new employee. "Her name is Elpithia Shackly, but you can call her Elpie. Elpie, if you don't mind, please stand up." Elpie stood and gave everyone a winning smile. She wore blue medical scrubs and looked like she came right out of central casting for a TV show no-nonsense ER nursing supervisor. She was in her mid-fifties, attractive, with short sandy brown hair that revealed a lean neck and strong jaw line. She not only lived by the book, she looked like she wrote the damned book.

In her job interview Phil made clear his expectations.

"Your title will be 'director,' but what I really need is a benevolent dictator," Phil told her. "Someone who will put that department back on its feet and pointed in the right direction. Can you do that?"

"I'll take that department apart and put it back together again if I have to," Elpie said. "Proper resident care is 'Job 1.' Don't you worry about a thing." Phil liked the sound of that.

"You're hired," he said. Here at the staff meeting he proudly introduced her to the Sanctuary team.

"She comes to us from St. Vincent Hospital, which recently won the Outstanding Patient Experience Award and the Critical Care Excellence Award. So, welcome aboard, Elpie." The room gave her a generous round of applause. He then cleared his throat to introduce his ambitious scheme.

"Last year at my Orlando facility we hosted a barn-busting event we called a 'Fall Festival.' It consisted of several events and exhibits over three days that drew literally thousands of people. In the front parking lot we hosted an antique car rally with food booths and refreshments. We arranged to have some amusement park rides for the kids, and lots of shade and benches for the grown-ups. Inside we held a senior fashion show using our own residents as runway models to feature the latest in women's wear with clothing on loan from the major garment stores in town. We hosted food competitions, including pies, cupcakes, and BBQ ribs."

"That sounds like a bit much," the food service director said.

"You're right," Phil admitted. "Maybe we'll just have a pie baking challenge." The staff all nodded in agreement.

"We asked various city officials to serve as judges, like the mayor, newspaper editor, high school principal, and police chief. Then we held a golf tournament at the local golf course restricted to seniors only, with a $1,000 first place cash prize. And finally, we held a huge arts and crafts competition in various categories, including quilting, knitting, painting, pottery, and woodworking."

The staff heaved a collective sigh at the enormity of this proposed undertaking.

"When are we going to do this?" Lester, the activities director, asked.

"We're going to do it right at the end of the Montana Fair – the first week of September. We'll run ads in all the newspapers in the region. We'll invite the governor, our two senators, and our congressman to attend." He turned to Susan Phillips, the marketing director.

"And Susan, I know we're going to be swamped with visitors, so I'm going to ask you to arrange for some of our residents to help out as tour guides." Then he turned to Abbey, the food service director.

"Abbey, I'm going to fatten your budget up for those three days, and I want some extra special meals for any guests who might want to dine with us. I'm talking shrimp scampi and lobster kind of meals." Abbey looked dizzy with delight at the thought of pulling out all the stops.

"These three days are going to put us on the map and under the microscope, but it's going to give us the platform we need to shine in the eyes of the public. There's no telling the good that will come from this. I'll be talking to each of you department heads individually for your specific assignments, but if you have any questions right now, fire away." Fran, the housekeeping director raised her hand with a smile.

"Yeah – when we're done with the fall festival, can we get back to solving the riddle of the sphinx?" The room broke up with laughter. Phil nodded and grinned.

# CHAPTER 26

When the meeting adjourned, Annie handed a note to Phil.

"Joe Henjum stopped by while we were in the staff meeting. He said he's going to the shooting range today and wanted to know if you cared to join."

"Absolutely. Find out when." While Phil made some calls to start the ball rolling on the Fall Festival, Annie spoke to Joe. She waited until Phil got off the phone.

"Joe said 1:00 p.m., but he wants you to stop by to choose your firearm." Phil grinned.

"Welcome to the wild west," he said.

"Don't shoot your foot off," Annie said. Phil walked down to Joe Henjum's apartment and knocked. The door opened.

"Come in," Joe said.

"Are you sure I can do this?" Phil asked.

"Have you ever fired a pistol before?" Joe asked.

"Never."

"Then it's high time you learned." He led Phil to his gun rack and lifted out his Marine issue M18 9mm automatic.

"This is what the Marines use now – it's a 9mm automatic. It's used by the Army, Navy, Air Force, and Coast Guard." He slid the magazine out and handed the pistol to Phil. Phil took it in his hand and felt its weight and smooth finish.

"How many bullets does the clip hold?" Phil asked.

"Seventeen in a standard clip – twenty-one in a modified clip," Joe said. He let Phil get acquainted with the M18, while he turned back to the gun rack to retrieve his M1911 single-action Colt .45 semi-automatic pistol.

"This is what we used in Vietnam," Joe said. "Seven bullets in the standard clip. They tested this model in the Chicago stockyards. The .45 slug knocks a steer off its feet on impact. It was the weapon of choice when the enemy got within fifteen to twenty-five yards."

"They got that close?" Phil said.

"In the jungle – sometimes hand-to-hand," Joe said. He collected the M18 from Phil and put the two automatic pistols in a travel bag, along with several boxes of cartridges. "I think because you've never fired one of these before, let's not start on a gun range. You'll just scare everybody to death and they might kick us out. I know a place about forty-five minutes north of Billings where we can just shoot up the hillside all by ourselves. I'll take some empty cans for targets, and we'll have a ball. Ready to go?"

"Let me change into something a little more rugged," Phil said. "I'll meet you in the lobby." Phil went upstairs and got into some jeans, boots, and a work shirt, then met Joe at the front door. Annie waved goodbye.

"Keep your phone on," she said.

Joe drove north on U.S. 87 about thirty miles. During the drive, Phil got some valuable one-on-one with his new Vietnam war hero.

"Would you mind sharing how you got your Medal of Honor ribbon?" Phil asked.

"I don't generally tell this story, 'cause it just feels like I'm cashing in on the fates of war, sparing me when a hundred other men died doing the very same thing."

"I understand, but a lot of those CMH ribbons were awarded posthumously. That tells me this award isn't given for surviving, it's given for valor. Maybe you can't tell their stories, but I'd like to hear yours," Phil said.

"Fair enough," Joe said. "It was 1970. I was part of a division assigned to fortify and defend Firebase Ripcord in the A Shau Valley. That firebase was set on four hilltops overlooking the valley and was used by the Marines to destroy NVA supply lines. On July 1 over 25,000 NVA surrounded the firebase and laid siege to it. We were outnumbered ten to one. The battle for the hilltops went on for twenty-three days. Every day we were losing men and running low on supplies. It was really only the high ground that kept the NVA from overrunning us.

"One night they tested the perimeter where my men were stationed. They must have thrown a couple hundred regulars at us. They broke through the lines and we were in the shit-storm of our lives. You couldn't tell who was who without night flares, and most of the fighting was hand-to-hand. When our platoon leader was killed in an ambush, I took command of the rifle company and led a counterattack down the hill and into the heart of the assault. We formed a perimeter around us and fought through the night. When we ran out of ammunition, we used the rifles of our dead comrades, then we grabbed rifles off the dead Viet Cong. When that ran out, we fought with knives, then stones. By morning, only five of us remained, every one of us wounded. But we stopped the assault. A hundred and thirty-eight Americans died defending that firebase. They handed out three Medals of Honor and five Distinguished Service medals to the men who fought in the battle of Firebase Ripcord. I was one of them."

The car was silent for the remainder of the drive to their destination. Around 2:00 they turned off U.S. 87 to a small service road and continued for a mile, where Joe pulled off and cut the engine.

"Here we are," Joe said. The wooded terrain presented scattered clusters of scrub brush, offering few natural breaks for a walking path. Joe tossed Phil the bag full of tin can targets, while he took the pistol and ammunition bag and walked through the woods for about fifty yards, where the forest broke into a clearing, revealing fallen tree trunks and wild grass.

"Set up a row of cans along that fallen tree," Joe said, pointing to a nearby dead scrub oak trunk. Phil lined up a dozen coffee and powdered milk cans. Joe laid out a small blanket with the pistols and ammunition on display.

"First, a few words of instruction," Joe said. "There's a lot of rules to firearms that I'm not going to bore you with, but there are a few essentials that will save your life and keep you from accidentally killing someone else."

"Yeah, those are the ones I want to hear," Phil said.

"OK – rule number one. If you forget everything else, do not forget this rule. Never point a gun at anything you do not intend to kill. Not for play, not for laughs, not even to scare someone. It doesn't matter if you are sure it is empty or not. You got that?"

"Got it."

"OK – let's get started," said Joe. He chose the M18 for Phil's first lesson. He slid out the clip to check its load – it was full. He put the clip in his pocket and gave the empty pistol to Phil.

"You don't need a loaded pistol right now. I'm going to show you how to handle and shoot this bad boy. After you shoot it for a while you'll learn how to adjust to its recoil. Just know that it's got a kick like a mule."

"Got it," Phil said.

"Just four things to remember to shoot this gun and hit your target," Joe began. "Proper grip, good sight alignment, proper trigger press, and proper body posture. I'll demonstrate these four tips for you right now." Joe took the M18 back from Phil and slid the clip in place, then turned to the tin cans lined up about twenty yards away. Using full arm extension, he calmly fired five shots one second apart – aim-fire, aim-fire, aim-fire, aim-fire, aim-fire – knocking down a can with each round.

"Now you try," Joe said. He handed the pistol to Phil, who took it as if he were handed a delicate baby chick.

"OK – now what do I do?' Phil asked.

"Grip the gun like I showed you," Joe said. "Trigger hand first, then opposite hand wrapping around for extra control and support." Phil did his best to imitate what Joe demonstrated. "Line up the sights. Place your leg opposite your trigger arm slightly back. And firmly pull the trigger." Phil obeyed and POW! He fired a pistol for the first time in his life. The gun kicked his arms up over his head, and he almost dropped his weapon. The bullet took a chunk of bark out of a tree ten feet away from the cans.

"Wow – how'd I do?" Phil said.

"Good start. We'll work on accuracy later."

For the next two hours they went through four boxes of cartridges, and Phil learned how to load a clip and get control of the recoil. Joe made sure that Phil hit a can before calling it quits for the day. It took all of two hours, but Phil felt like Wyatt Earp at the end of the session.

On the drive back, Phil took stock of his emotional state.

"I feel so keyed up right now. My heart's pounding. What's that all about?" Phil said.

"It's the feel of all that power in your hands. You're not used to it. It's exhilarating and scary all at the same time. It takes a little time for your brain to adjust so you can focus."

Phil just sighed and stared out the window at the wide open wilderness.

# CHAPTER 27

Joe and Phil stopped for dinner at the north end of Billings, then pulled into the parking lot of The Sanctuary about 7:00 p.m.

"Thanks for this day. It really lifted my spirits," Joe said.

"I'm the one who should thank you – for everything," Phil said.

Annie met them both at the front door. She rarely stayed that late, and Phil thought she just couldn't wait to hear how the day went. But one look in her eyes and he knew something was wrong. Joe waved good bye to both of them and continued to his apartment.

"What's wrong?' Phil asked.

"Joe's wife passed away today," she said.

"Oh, no," Phil said.

"They've been waiting at the hospital for you guys to get back so they could let him know."

"I'll tell him. And I'll take him over to the hospital. He shouldn't try to do this alone."

"All right – I'll tell them you're coming."

Phil made that long lonely walk to Joe's apartment to break the saddest news a manager can share with a resident, the toughest part of his job. When he told Joe the tragic news of his wife's passing, Joe tried to maintain his composure in true military style, but his heart simply burst from the pain. He sat in his lounger and wept.

"Let me take you to the hospital, so you can see her," Phil said.

"They're holding her there, waiting for your instructions." Joe nodded without a word. He grabbed his coat and followed Phil to his car. The hospital nurses knew Joe from his nearly daily visits to see his wife. They surrounded him with love and comfort as he filled out the paperwork for his choice of funeral homes.

"Is there a special dress you'd like for her to wear?" one nurse asked. Joe just nodded, his eyes too full of tears and his heart overcome with grief.

"I'll come by tomorrow and get it," the nurse said. Phil took Joe back to The Sanctuary and made sure he was OK for the night.

"I'll check on you in the morning," Phil said.

What a horrible end to such a joyful day, Phil thought, as he walked to his apartment. His heart ached for Joe, and he struggled to come up with something he might do to assuage Joe's pain. Late into the night his brain toiled. And then it came to him. Despite the late hour, he called Annie.

"I need you to order two airline tickets for me and Joe," Phil said. "The funeral is on Thursday. We'll leave Friday morning."

"Where are you going?" Annie said.

"We're going to Washington, D.C. And don't tell Joe. I want it to be a surprise."

The funeral chapel filled to overflowing on Thursday. Joe was revered in both the military community and the general public, both a hero and a legend with fellow Marines. The newspaper printed a glowing tribute to his wife in the obituary column, and the Billings American Legion Post 4 and Post 117 attended the service in full uniform.

At the end of the service and interment, Phil drove Joe back to The Sanctuary.

"I'm tired," Joe said. "I think I'll just turn in." Phil was tempted to break the news about the excursion he had planned for the two of them the very next day, but he wanted to wait until Annie got the itinerary and boarding passes printed out. He left Joe and went straight to the office, where Annie just pressed the PRINT command button.

When Phil left, Joe slowly walked over to his gun cabinet and pulled out his M18 9mm pistol, checked the clip, and went to his lounger. For several minutes he studied his gun, considered his pain and the long road ahead without his loving wife. He cocked the pistol and put the barrel in his mouth.

"Here's the boarding passes and hotel reservations," Annie said.

"Great," Phil said. "I'm going to let Joe know right now. He'll be so surprised."

Joe let the barrel of his gun rest on his tongue for several minutes. The taste of metal and oil combined to create an unpleasant flavor, salty and acidic. He moved his thumb to the trigger and held it there for one last moment. Suddenly he heard a knock at the door. He ignored it. Probably the housekeeper, he thought. Then the knock escalated in volume and urgency.

"Joe – this is Phil. Can I come in?" When Phil heard no reply, he assumed Joe had already gone to bed. He reached for his master key and unlocked the door. He walked into the apartment and saw Joe in his lounger with his M18 sitting in his lap. In a heartbeat Phil sized up the situation.

"You checking out?" Phil said calmly.

"Any reason why I shouldn't?" Joe said.

"Yeah – about 50,000 reasons. Isn't that about the number of names engraved on The Wall?"

"Fifty-eight thousand three hundred twenty," Joe said, "to be exact."

"Why don't you check with them first. I think they might have something to say about it," Phil said. He slowly walked up and laid the flight information on Joe's lap. "We're going there tomorrow." Joe took his hand off the gun and picked up the itinerary. Phil lifted the M18 from Joe's lap and removed the clip like an old pro.

"I don't think you need this," Phil said. "I'll pick you up tomorrow morning at 6:30. Our flight leaves at 8:00."

The flight took them from Billings to Minneapolis, and from Minneapolis to Reagan International, on the shores of the Potomac

River. The view of the Capitol Mall with the iconic Washington Monument stirred Joe's loins. They collected their bags and hailed a taxi.

"Take us to the Hyatt Place on the National Mall," Phil said. Within fifteen minutes they pulled up to the elegant Hyatt Place, only four blocks south of the Mall and the Capitol Building.

"Branson, party of two," Phil told the front desk.

"Yes, Mr. Branson, we have two rooms on the tenth floor. You'll be staying two nights?"

"I think so, but you never know," Phil said. The desk clerk gave them card keys for each room.

"Will you be dining in tonight?" the clerk asked.

"Can we get a table for two at 7:00?" Phil asked. The clerk gave her computer screen a quick look.

"That will be no problem." Phil turned to Joe.

"We've got a full day tomorrow. It might be good to just eat here and turn in early. What do you think?"

"You're in charge," Joe said. Phil turned back to the clerk.

"Done."

The filet mignon just melted in Phil's mouth, and Joe's beef bourguignon couldn't have tasted better if it were prepared for the King of England. After a Sazerac night cap, the two called it a night.

In the morning, Phil met Joe in the dining room for a light breakfast and a strategy summit to finalize the day's activities.

"I say we ease ourselves gently into this whirlwind tour. Let's start at the Marine Memorial to give us the proper historical spring-board for our journey. Then I suggest we move to the World War II Memorial. After that, we break for lunch at Hill Country Barbeque on 7th Street for the world's absolute best beef ribs you'll ever wrap your lips around. Then we'll head over to the Three Soldiers Memorial, and finish the day at The Wall. How's that sound?" said Phil.

"This is my first and probably last time here, so let's just make the most of the day," Joe said. They shook hands and stepped outside to flag a taxi.

"The Marine Memorial, please," Phil said. Across town, over the Potomac River, and into Arlington they drove to the sacred grounds abutting the Arlington National Cemetery, where the Marine Corps Sculpture stood, capturing that moment in time when a small band of heroic Marines planted the American flag atop Mt. Suribachi on the island of Iwo Jima. Around the base of the statue, at the top of the pedestal, were engraved every major U.S. Marine engagement from the Revolutionary War to Iraq. An inscription at the base read:

> *Dedicated To The Marine Dead Of All Wars,*
> *And Their Comrades Of Other Services*
> *Who Fell Fighting Beside Them.*

Joe slowly walked around the memorial, reading the names of every Marine engagement, forty-five in all, from 1775 to the present – 245 years in which the Marines answered the call to defend a nation in peril. Phil stood back to allow Joe time and space to absorb the emotional impact of this hallowed shrine and a brotherhood to which he belonged. Busloads of tourists milled around the site, with children scampering about, oblivious to the import of this monument. Joe sat on a bench for an hour to meditate. He walked over to Phil.

"Helluva monument. I'm done. Let's go," Joe said. Phil nodded. They boarded a taxi for the World War II Memorial in the heart of the Capitol Mall, at the east end of the Reflecting Pool. They stepped with reverence into the fountain area surrounded by marble pillars, each supporting a wreath, commemorating every major battle fought in World War II. Joe was born near the war's end, in 1944, but his father fought and died in the Battle of Okinawa, in April 1945. Joe sat beside that pillar and grieved the loss of his father. From there, the two walked over to the Washington Monument, a towering 555-foot Egyptian obelisk, the tallest monumental column in the world. Joe admired the Capitol Building in the far distance, with its enormous Greek-inspired dome. Then he turned his gaze to the west at the awesome Lincoln Memorial. It was almost too much to take in, the enormity of it all.

"It's time for lunch," Phil said. At Hill Country BBQ, Joe and Phil enjoyed the tenderest, most succulent beef ribs known to man, along with a bevy of side dishes and fixin's. Joe chose the green bean casserole and Phil favored the mac-and-cheese and baked beans. The meal almost put them into noontime stupor, but they soldiered on. Next stop – *The Three Soldiers.*

At the western edge of The Wall, a larger-than-life bronze statue of three Vietnam soldiers in battle gear, stood brave and tall, each representing a different race (African, European, and Hispanic), looking over their right shoulder back at The Wall, symbolizing, among other things, the survivors of that war as they look back at the fallen. When Joe approached this memorial he felt his knees buckle. The agony of his own journey home, leaving behind so many fallen comrades, washed over him with a sadness he tried to bury forty-five years ago. He stood beside the statue and looked over his own right shoulder to see The Wall in the near distance and knew it was time for this long overdue reunion.

Joe and Phil walked over to the western edge of the The Wall, a collection of 144 granite panels inscribed with the names of every soldier who died in that conflict, from 1959 to 1975, each name in chronological order from left to right. Joe scanned each panel with reverence and noted the many gifts and tokens left behind by loved ones, from bouquets to letters, to unopened bottles of whiskey. He heard that a few years earlier someone even left a brand new Harley Davidson Motorcycle behind as a gift for his fallen buddy. Joe gravitated to the 1970 panel where he fought his last battle at Firebase Ripcord. On that panel he touched the engravings of dear friends who perished. He laid both hands against the panel and asked forgiveness for surviving while they died. From the fog of time he heard them call back, "Go home and enjoy the life we cannot share. Live it for us."

Joe lingered at The Wall, communing with his brothers, until sundown, when he could see their names no more, and said good bye with purpose new. He confessed to Phil that the day wrung him out like a rag, depleted and drained of regret unforgiven, now at last released to torture him no more.

"Take me home. I want to live," he said soft as a prayer.

# CHAPTER 28

On Monday morning Phil managed to convince Sidney Howell to bring his Elvis show back to The Sanctuary for the Fall Festival for a special encore performance. He promised a massive turnout and fawning news coverage, just what an insecure entertainer needs to hear. Annie stuck her head in his office door.

"Mrs. Angler is here to see you," she said.

"Send her in," Phil said. He stood to greet her and invited her to sit down. He knew she must be devastated at the mysterious disappearance of Walter, but had no idea what she might want of him.

"I'm so sorry about Walter's disappearance. Have you heard anything from him?" he asked. Clara pulled out the small box and the puzzling pen that showed up at the house a few days after Walter's exodus.

"Funny you should say that. I got this box in the mail a couple of days after Walter left to go meet someone," she said. She lifted the pen out of the box. "It had this large pen inside. I didn't know where it came from – the return address on the box was our own home address, as if we mailed it to ourselves. I tossed the box in our trash can in the den and left the pen on the desk. But yesterday I was in the den looking for something to write with and suddenly thought of that pen. I picked it up and saw a button on the side. I thought it was some new-fangled way to reveal the ballpoint tip, but instead it played a message. Listen –" She pushed the button and the recorded message played—

> *What do you think?*
> *I don't like it. She could put us all in jail.*
> *What do we do?*
> *We have to make sure she doesn't talk. Ever.*

"Does that mean anything to you?" Clara asked.

"It might. We both recognize one of those voices was Walter," Phil said. Clara lifted out a piece of paper that had been tucked tightly inside the lid of the box.

"I found this note inside the lid of the box," Clara said. "I didn't notice it at first, and even tossed it in the trash can. But when I heard this recording, I thought there might have been a message or an explanation of some kind that I overlooked. I searched through the trash and found the box, and this note tucked inside." Phil opened the handwritten note. It read simply—

> *Please give this box to Sgt. Belvedere.*

"I'll see that he gets it," Phil said.

"All right. Thank you. I hope it helps," Clara said.

"I'm sure it will," Phil said.

"I never understood why he left his car at the Rimrock Mall," Clara said out loud, almost to herself, as she rose to leave. That name suddenly rang a bell for Phil. That was where Sylvia was found dead.

"How did you know his car was left at the mall?"

"The towing service told me that's where it was." She clutched her purse and said good bye. Phil got on the phone.

"This is Sergeant Belvedere," the voice on the other end said.

"Mike, this is Phil over at The Sanctuary. I got something over here you are going to want to hear."

"I'll be right over."

Mike arrived in about twenty minutes, and Annie showed him into Phil's office, where Phil sat waiting.

"Have a seat," Phil said. "I just got this from Mrs. Angler just a half hour ago." He lifted the pen out of the box. "Walter mailed it to himself. Listen to this." He pushed the small PLAY button.

> *What do you think?*
> *I don't like it. She could put us all in jail.*
> *What do we do?*
> *We have to make sure she doesn't talk. Ever.*

"I recognize Walter's voice," Mike said, "but who is the other?" Mike said.

"That's Darryl Brooks, our company's Director of Operations."

"Who do you think they're talking about?" Mike said.

"I'll tell you what I think. I think they're talking about Sylvia, and Walter recorded that conversation with this little recording pen, maybe for blackmail or maybe just for insurance."

"Makes sense," Mike said.

"Mrs. Angler told me that Walter left the house to meet with someone, and that was the last time she saw him. Then just now in my office she told me that his car was found abandoned at the Rimrock Mall. Isn't that where Sylvia was found?"

"Yeah."

"Aren't there surveillance cameras filming the parking lot?" Suddenly the light went on in Mike's brain.

"Of course. If he met somebody in that parking lot, it'll be on film. You know where his car was parked?" Mikes said.

"We can find out," Phil said. He called the City Towing service and gave the receiver to Mike.

"This is Sergeant Belvedere with the Billings Police. I understand you towed a car from the Rimrock Mall on July 27. It would have been a dark blue Lincoln Continental."

"Yeah, they came by and picked it up yesterday," the receptionist said.

"Can you check the file and see where the car was located exactly?" Mike said.

"Let me pull the file," the receptionist said.

"It was in the northside parking lot," she said. Mike thanked her and hung up, then looked at Phil.

"I say we go talk to the Mall Security people," Phil said.

"You take your car – I'll meet you there," Mike said.

They found the mall management office and Mike flashed his badge.

"We need to see the security footage for the northside parking lot on July 24," Mike said.

"The whole day?" the receptionist said.

"Just from noon on," Mike said. The receptionist located the disc for July 24 and dropped it in the player, then fast forwarded to the afternoon of July 24.

"OK, keep on fast forwarding," Mike said. "We are looking to see when a navy blue Lincoln Continental parked under that lamp post," he said, pointing to the screen.

"All right," the receptionist said, and kept her finger on the fast forward until they saw the Lincoln Continental roll in at 4:45 p.m. and park.

"There it is," Phil said, pointing. The receptionist stopped the machine and then pushed PLAY. They watched as Walter sat waiting for Darryl Brooks to arrive. At 5:00 p.m. Darryl's Pontiac Grand Prix rolled up alongside Walter's Lincoln Continental.

"OK – freeze that," Mike said. "Now, can you zoom in on the license plate?"

"Sure," the receptionist said. She focused in on the front plate and zoomed in until the plate filled the entire screen.

"Illinois plates," Phil said. "That's Darryl's car." Mike wrote the license number down and dialed his cell phone.

"Yeah, hi, Earl, this is Mike. I need you to run down an Illinois plate for me." He read off the seven serial number characters to Earl. "Let me know who that's registered to. OK, thanks." He hung up and got back to watching the video.

"From this angle I can't really see the driver of the Grand Prix through the windshield," Phil said. Then they watched Walter get out of his car and walk over to the Grand Prix, pausing to look up at the surveillance camera.

"Look at that," Phil said. "It's almost like he knew he was being filmed and wanted us to ID him."

"Yeah, seems that way," Mike said. They watched the Grand Prix for about three minutes when they saw the reflection of two muzzle flashes through the windshield.

"Did you see that?" Phil said. "What was that?" Mike hit the PAUSE button on the player and turned to the receptionist.

"Would you excuse us for a few minutes?" he said. The receptionist nodded and left the room. Mike turned back to Phil.

"It looked like two gunshots, if you ask me," Mike said.

"Holy shit, are you telling me Darryl shot Walter?" Phil said. Mike did not answer, but stared at the screen to see what would happen next. He hit the PLAY button to resume the action. From the dashboard windshield it looked like a blanket was thrown over Walter and the Grand Prix pulled out of the parking lot and out of the camera's view, leaving the Lincoln Continental behind. Mike hit the STOP button just as his cell phone rang.

"Yeah, this is Mike – OK – all right, thanks." He hung up.

"That was Sergeant Holick. That Grand Prix is registered to Darryl Brooks," Mike said.

"I guess that explains what happened to Walter," Phil said.

"We're a long way from charging Darryl Brooks with anything," Mike said.

"What do you mean? You just said the Grand Prix is his car."

"Did you see Darryl through the windshield? Because I didn't."

"Well, who else could it be?"

"That's not the point," Mike said. "I've got to be able to put him at the scene – not just his car. See, I could ask him where he was on July 24 and he could say he was home sick, and his wife might even back his story up. I could prove his car was in Billings, and he could say it was stolen. You see? I gotta prove he was here," Mike said.

"OK, so how do we do that?" Phil said.

"Well, let's think about this," Mike said. "If Darryl drove here from Chicago, he probably didn't take the freeway – too much of a chance of getting stopped. He probably took a secondary route, I'm guessing U.S. Highway 12. And he probably paid for his gas with cash to avoid a paper trail. But if he paid with cash, he had to go inside the gas station, and most gas stations today have surveillance cameras behind the cash register in case of robberies. So, if we could find just one gas station he stopped at, we might get lucky and catch him on tape. And the closer to Billings the better."

"But, it's like 1,600 miles between here and Chicago. You know how many gas stations that is?" Phil said.

"More than a few," Mike said. "But we should be able to narrow a few things down."

"How?" Phil asked.

"A Grand Prix has a tank capacity of about seventeen gallons, and on the highway it gets maybe twenty-eight miles per gallon. That's about 400 miles per tank. So, if he left Chicago on a full tank, he only stopped three, maybe four times for gas."

"Yeah, OK." Phil said.

"I'll have Earl retrace his route along Highway 12, leaving Billings and going east. It's pretty rural – a lot of farmland and not many gas stations. And, just in case he wasn't as smart as I'm giving him credit for, I'll take I-90 and check all the gas stations between here and the Wyoming state line. Maybe one of us will get lucky."

"Anything you need me to do?" Phil asked.

"Not just yet," Mike said. He held out the recorder pen. "You've already done plenty. I'm going to hang onto this pen for the time being. You just get back to work. I'll let you know if I need anything."

The next day Mike and Earl got busy. Mike took I-90. Between Billings and the Wyoming state line there were thirteen offramps, with gas stations operating on only four of them. The first one was the Hardin exit, thirty miles east of Billings. Earl went north on U.S. 87 from Billings, then veered off on Highway 12, where an Exxon station and a Casey's Corner convenience store operated 24/7. No luck there. The next gas station was five miles farther east, at "Five Corners". Earl pulled into another affiliated Casey's Corner convenience store, where "Liberty Gas" was sold.

Mike just finished his first stop along I-90 at the Hardin exit, when his cell phone rang.

"This is Mike."

"Bingo," Earl said.

Mike drove up to Five Corners and met Earl at the convenience store. They watched the footage of Darryl paying for gas.

"Well, that seals it," Earl said.

"We still need a body," Mike said. "If he's driving back home on Highway 12, he's going to want to dump that body before he gets into a big city. Just to cover our bases, let's send out a wire to every police station between Billings and the Missouri River. We want to know about any unidentified male bodies found anywhere along Highway 12."

# CHAPTER 29

On Thursday morning Annie popped her head in Phil's office to say good morning.

"Morning, boss." She saw his head buried in a brochure on Yellowstone. He lowered the brochure enough to make eye contact.

"I'm looking for something to do this weekend. You ever been to Yellowstone?" he said.

"That's like asking someone from Anaheim if they've ever been to Disneyland," Annie said.

"I've never been to Anaheim or Disneyland. So, would that be a 'yes' or a 'no'?" Phil said.

"You've never been to Disneyland?" Annie said.

"Never had the pleasure. I've been to Disney World in Orlando," Phil said. "Does that qualify?"

"What am I going to do with you? That's like saying you grew up on chuck steak and never bothered to try prime rib."

"We can debate my dietary preferences some other time. I just want to get your take on Yellowstone. I figured since I'm in the neighborhood, I should go check it out."

"By yourself?"

"Sure – why not?"

"Don't even think about it. I practically grew up in Yellowstone. I'm not doing anything this weekend. I'll give you the insider's tour." Phil appreciated Annie's sass and brass, but the optics of the boss and office manager fraternizing off the clock could cause grumbling among the troops.

"That might create a little conflict," Phil said. "Don't you think?"

"I won't tell if you won't."

"It'll be overnight," Phil said.

"I know just the place," Annie said.

"Are you sure?"

"Trust me. I got this." Phil had been around enough to recognize professional quicksand when he saw it.

"All right, but can we just keep this little excursion between us? I don't want to read about it in the facility newsletter." Annie grinned.

"As long as you behave yourself, I can be discreet."

"OK. I'll pick you up at your house tomorrow after lunch."

"You know where I live?"

"Yep. Me, the company, and the IRS, we all know where you live."

Friday around 1:30 Phil pulled his Suburban into Annie's driveway and honked. She skipped out the front door in jeans, boots, cowgirl shirt and hat, with a small suitcase in hand.

"I didn't pack a sidearm. Do you think I'll need it?" she said and she climbed into the passenger seat. Phil smiled.

"I'm not planning on shooting our dinner. I thought we'd just buy it," Phil said. He pointed the Suburban toward I-90 west.

"I figured we'd get off the freeway at Livingston and go south on 89 to Gardiner," Phil said.

"Absolutely not. That's for rookies. Get off on Highway 212 just past Laurel. We're going in through the Beartooth Mountains," Annie said. Phil happily complied, taken by Annie's adventurous spirit. As they drove, Phil made small talk.

"Your folks live in Billings?" he asked.

"They live in Florida – one of those Del Webb communities. They got sick of the snow. My grandma lives here. They tried to talk her into moving down with them, but she knows everybody here in town. She doesn't want to leave."

"So, she lives alone?"

"Yeah, Grandpa died of a heart attack a few years back, so it's just Grandma in that great big house. I tried to talk her into moving here, but she said she wasn't ready, like it was some kinda punishment."

"Could she afford it?"

"Yeah. If she sold her house, she could live off that, plus her savings and social security till the second coming."

"Now, I know the Yellowstone River runs through Billings," Phil said, "but is that just a namesake, or does that river literally come down from Yellowstone?"

"It literally comes down from Yellowstone Lake – you'll see."

U.S. Highway 212 split off from I-90 about fifteen miles west of Billings. The vista opened up to reveal a broad valley framed by the Beartooth Mountains to the west and the Pryor Mountain to the east. The stunning scenery with craggy mountains and shimmering aspen trees made the journey breathtaking.

"I got two rooms for us at the Pollard Hotel in Red Lodge," Annie said. "Wait till you see it. It's Montana history."

"Really?" Phil said.

"It was built in 1893, and it's got a who's who list of famous people who spent the night there."

"Like who?"

"Buffalo Bill Cody, William Jennings Bryant, Calamity Jane. It's a landmark." They rolled into Red Lodge about 4:00 p.m., right on Highway 212, and checked in. The hotel lobby looked like they had stepped out of a time machine to the turn of the twentieth century. Walls were paneled in hand-oiled pine, brass fixtures that gave off a golden shine, the heads of wild game mounted on the walls, and details of the past, from vintage furniture and lamps to window treatments, to remind guests of the standard of elegance in 1900.

"Let's go for a walk around town," Annie said.

"Yeah, I'd like to check this town out," Phil said. They walked past galleries, steak houses, gift shops, western clothing stores, all with that distinctive western ambiance Montanans are known for. Red Lodge Mountain and Grizzly Peak to the west cast a giant shadow over the town as the sun slipped behind these craggy buttes.

Dinner in the hotel included live entertainment with a special appearance of the Big Sky Boys, a local favorite, yodeling and harmonizing some of the classics, from "Ghost Riders in the Sky" to Marty Robbins' "El Paso." The extensive wine list provided a blush red vintage for every palate. Phil attempted to conquer the house favorite, a twenty-four-ounce porterhouse, cooked to a medium pink and topped with a pad of melting butter, but he surrendered halfway to the summit of this Mt. Everest of steaks. Annie settled for a petite six-ounce filet. As Phil paused from his monster steak to catch his breath, he watched Annie busying herself with her own meal. Although he had eaten meals with her before, he never noticed how Annie used her knife, cutting the steak with her right hand, then switching the knife to her left hand so she could move the fork to her right hand to feed herself. He smiled.

"You use a knife the same way my wife did," Phil said.

"What do you mean?"

"You use both your knife and fork with your right hand."

"Doesn't everybody?"

"No. I use my knife with my left hand but use my fork with my right hand." Annie shrugged.

"Didn't know there was a right and wrong way to do it," she said. Phil chuckled.

"There's no wrong way. It just tickled me. Kind of endearing."

The Big Sky Boys offered up a few plaintive love songs, prompting two or three couples to take to the small dance floor. Phil stood and offered his hand to Annie.

"Care to dance?" Phil said. Annie took notice of the beat of the music – it sure wasn't a lively two-step, it was slow and soulful. She decided she was ready for some up-close dancing. She gave Phil her hand and they joined the others. Now it was Phil's turn to lead. He took Annie in his arms and gently brought her close – too close to look into each other's eyes. She felt his confidence in this type of dance and let him guide her as he wished, with easy side steps, gentle twirls, and soft swaying. She felt comfortable in his arms and sensed his subtle cues, with an open hand, a raised arm, a delicate nudge.

To onlookers they appeared seasoned partners engaged in a choreographed routine, Red Lodge's version of Fred Astaire and Ginger Rogers. When the song ended, the patrons in the room gave them a polite round of applause. The clapping suddenly roused Annie from the fantasy she had drifted into. She gathered herself and looked into Phil's eyes, who returned the glance. They held their gaze long past the rules of courtesy, then turned back to their table.

After dinner they relaxed in the parlor before turning in.

"I feel like I'm not just in another place but I'm in another time. It's all very stirring," Phil said.

"I feel the same way," Annie said. "I think I'll just say good night."

In the morning, after a light breakfast, they hit the road south to scale the winding route up the Beartooth Range, past Granite Peak, the highest elevation in Montana, at 12,807 feet. In the distance they spotted the sharply pointed spire after which the mountain took its name, for its resemblance of a bear's long and narrow fang.

"This is the northeast entrance to Yellowstone," Annie said. "In the winter this road is closed because of all the snow. So, this is a treat."

Crossing over into Wyoming, the road took them to the modest Top of The World gift shop, at 9,400-foot elevation. The 360-degree view of the earth's crust left Phil speechless.

"You need to buy a T-shirt to remember this place," Annie said.

"Oh, trust me – I'm not going to forget this," Phil said.

In another ninety miles they stood at the observation deck for the Yellowstone Lower Falls. This thundering waterfall sent vast cascades of water down a deep ravine and into a massive gorge, forcing a mist into the air that created continuous rainbows. In a moment an eagle took flight, catching an updraft and floating from one side of the gorge to the other. Annie pointed to it.

"Did you see that?"

"Yeah – that's something you won't see in Orlando," Phil whispered. He felt unable to move, his senses overwhelmed at the magnitude of nature urgently at work. Nothing in his brief walk on this earth compared – not the timid ocean waves on a Florida shore, the quiet serenity of the Everglades, or even the stately view from a lighthouse along the Outer Banks. He felt small in this swirling landscape.

"Hungry yet?" Annie said.

"Yeah, I could eat," Phil said.

They followed the road past a small herd of free-range bison out for a stroll, who ruled the road by park policy and their enormous heft. Should an angry bison choose to square off with a four-door sedan, the outcome would be uncertain.

Phil settled for a bison burger at the Yellowstone Lodge Restaurant, where it appeared humans had the last say. Buffalo, deer, elk, wild boar, and cow beef burgers, steaks, and roasts all topped the menu, providing delicacies of the old west for today's would-be mountain man.

"I may sound like a damned tourist, but I'm not leaving until I see Old Faithful," Phil said.

"That's our next stop," Annie said.

Before long they stood a mere fifty yards from the most famous geyser on earth. Park rangers mingled among the crowds, answering the same questions posed by visitors since the park first opened in 1872. Soon that old familiar rumble told everyone the geyser was about to blow. Phil and Annie watched as nature blew a plume of water 130 feet into the sky that lasted for three minutes. Phil watched in awe.

"That alone was worth the price of admission," Phil said.

"We've got reservations at the Canyon Village Lodge, but before we check in, I've got one more thing to show you," Annie said. They journeyed up the road to the famous Yellowstone mud pots – bubbling, splattering, gurgling, and reeking of steaming sulphur. Phil held his nose as they meandered along the plank walkways.

"I probably could have skipped this part," Phil said. "I'm not too sure about the spectator value of all this."

Yellowstone's sprawling three-story Canyon Village Lodge loomed grand and stately, with over 500 hotel rooms, restaurant, and gift shop. Phil and Annie checked into their rooms and got settled, then ventured to the restaurant for dinner. The menu offered a wide range of dishes, from Prime Rib to Alaska Salmon, New York Strip steak, Natural Chicken, and Grilled Quail.

"Quail?" Phil said. "We don't get much quail down in Florida. I might have to try that." Annie chose the Alaska Salmon, with roasted tomato relish, wild rice pilaf, chopped scallions, toasted sesame seeds, and seasonal vegetables.

"I doubt Lewis and Clark ate this good when they rolled through here," Phil said. After dinner, the two sat outside the lodge for some star-gazing. The cloudless nighttime sky offered a shimmering starry spectacle.

"It's hard to find a place in Orlando where the city lights don't drown out the constellations," Phil said. Annie felt that she already had enough stars in her eyes – she didn't need to look up into the heavens.

"Are you going back to Florida when you get The Sanctuary back on its feet?" Annie said.

"I don't know. When I took on this job, I only agreed to six months. But Montana is starting to grow on me."

"Just Montana?" she asked. Phil looked down at Annie's open hand, waiting, inviting. He slowly reached over and took it in his hand, then looked her in the eye.

"No, not just Montana. I'm getting partial to quail, too." Annie pulled her hand away and slapped his shoulder. He chuckled, then caught her arm and pulled her in. "Among other things," he added, then he kissed her. Her lips were soft and warm and tasted like plum nectar. He thought to keep the kiss short and sweet, but Annie hungered for more. She gently wrapped her hand around the back of his neck to let him know she was not nearly done. He happily surrendered.

# CHAPTER 30

Darryl Brooks just returned from a lunch meeting along Lakeshore Drive, when he walked past two men in suits waiting outside his splashy office. Susan, his sleek and elegant secretary, waved him over to her desk.

"These gentlemen are with the Chicago Police Department. They want to talk to you. I told them you were at lunch, but they said they'd wait." Darryl gave a quick look at the two men seated.

"Did they say what it's about?" Darryl said.

"No."

"OK. Give me a minute, then send them in," Darryl said. Darryl turned to his office. Susan walked over to the waiting guests.

"Can I get you anything to drink?"

"No, thank you. We're fine," one of the men said. She looked back at Darryl's office door.

"OK. I think he'll see you now," she said. The two men rose and followed Susan over to the office door. She tapped on the door, then opened it slightly.

"Are you ready?" she asked.

"Yes. Show them in," Darryl said. She opened the door wide and waved the two men in. "You can close the door behind you," Darryl said. The detectives took a moment to drink in the view from the twentieth floor of United Senior Living Corporation. Darryl approached the two men.

"Helluva view from up here. We don't get to see Chicago from this angle very often," one of them said. Darryl smiled politely.

"Darryl Brooks. I'm the Director of Operations for our fifty-two retirement communities across the country." He shook hands with both.

"I appreciate you taking time to see us," Alex said. They both produced their badges. "I'm Detective Alex Reynolds and this is Detective Ray Clemons with the Chicago Police. We wondered if you had a few minutes to answer a couple questions?"

"Sure. What's this about?"

"We're following up on a missing person out of Billings, Montana, and we were told you might be able to help," Alex said. Darryl waved them over to a small conference table in the room, and the three sat down.

"And why would I know about anyone missing in Montana?" Darryl said.

"Well, we understand he used to work for you. His name was Walter Angler. Do you know him?" Alex said.

"Yes, you're right. Walter was one of our facility managers out in Montana. The facility is called The Sanctuary, in Billings. But he's been retired for several months," Darryl said. "He might be busy touring Europe with his wife."

"When was the last time you saw him?" Ray said.

"I flew out there for his retirement party last February, I believe," Darryl said.

"And you haven't seen him since?" Alex said.

"No."

"Spoken to him over the phone since then?" Alex said. Darryl had to think about that.

"No."

"When you spoke to him last, did he seem distraught or distressed? Maybe suicidal?" Ray said.

"No. He seemed happy to retire."

"Can you account for your whereabouts on July 24?" Alex said.

The precision of that question raised a red flag in Darryl's mind. That was the actual day he met with Walter in the Rimrock Mall parking lot. But how could they know that? he thought.

"I'm not sure. Let me check my calendar." He pulled out his appointment book and flipped through the pages. July 24 was blank.

"Oh, yes, I remember. I was home that day, catching up on correspondence."

"You were here in Chicago all day on the twenty-fourth?" Alex rephrased the question just to be clear.

"Yes, all day, I was in my home, here in Chicago."

"And would anyone be able to confirm that?" Ray said.

"Sure. You can ask my wife. She was home all day as well."

"Anyone besides her? A neighbor maybe?" Ray said.

"No, I was inside all day."

"What kind of car do you drive?" Alex said.

"A Pontiac Grand Prix."

"Plate number?" Alex pressed. Darryl listed off the seven number characters on his plate, as the hackles on the back of his neck began to rise.

"When you were home on July 24, did anybody borrow your car for any reason?" Ray said.

"No. Why do you ask?" Darryl said. This line of questioning was becoming rather invasive, Darryl thought, and he didn't care for it.

"Just routine," Alex said.

"Is that all, because I need to get back to work," Darryl said. Alex and Ray exchanged glances. Alex checked his note pad to be sure.

"Yeah, I think that covers it," Alex said. They rose to leave, when Alex stopped short.

"Oh, one last question – do you know a Sylvia Longwood?"

"Why? Is she missing, too?" Darryl said.

"No," Alex said. Darryl searched his brain to be sure he did not misspeak.

"No, I don't believe I know her."

"She worked for you at The Sanctuary," Alex said.

"There's probably sixty other employees at that facility, and I don't know their names either."

"Of course. And why should you?" Alex said. The two detectives turned to leave.

"Will you be in town for the next few days if we have any follow-up questions?" Alex said.

"Sure. Happy to help," Darryl said. When they left, Darryl quickly dialed his home phone.

"Hi, sweetheart, just listen. I need you to do something for me…You might get a call today from someone claiming to be a detective from the Chicago Police…I know…No, nothing's wrong, it's just a guy from the office trying to win a bet. He might even show up at the house flashing a badge…Yeah, he's going to ask you if you and I were home all day on July 24. If he does, just tell him that we were…Yeah, I know I was gone, but you can't tell him that or I'll win the bet…That's the thing…Yeah, OK, good girl. I'll be home in time for dinner…I love you too."

# CHAPTER 31

The Montana Fair and Rodeo takes place every August in Billings, the largest such festival in all of Montana. The nine-day event occurs on the massive grounds of the MetraPark event center. Each year it draws over 250,000 visitors from all over the state and the surrounding region. The fair offers something for everyone. The main pavilion houses dozens of vendor booths selling food, clothing, cookware, outdoor furniture, books, and a host of other specialty items. Outside, the midway fun zone features carnival rides and numerous food stations, featuring corn dogs, BBQ, corn on the cob, fresh lemonade, and cotton candy. Stages around the grounds offer free entertainment that includes music, comedy, hypnosis, kids' entertainment, variety acts, draft horses, and more. The Pro Rodeo Area hosts rodeo competitions nightly.

Seniors at The Sanctuary loved the chance to visit the fair each day, and the facility shuttle bus made trips back and forth every hour. While some of the more frail residents skipped the event, they watched highlights of the fair on local TV channels.

Phil wanted to extend a personal invitation to Joe Henjum to join him in the VIP seating area to watch the bull riding competition. He stopped by Joe's apartment and knocked on the door.

"Come in," Joe said. Phil stepped in and saw Joe seated in his lounger, calm, motionless, staring at the ceiling.

"I got VIP tickets for the rodeo tonight, and you're coming

with me," Phil said. Joe's eyes wandered across the ceiling.

"I just came back from the doctor," Joe said evenly. "I got cancer." Suddenly, the air in Phil's party balloon deflated.

"When did this happen?" Phil said.

"I been feeling short of breath for a few weeks now and figured it must be some upper respiratory thing. I went to the doctor yesterday and he took some x-rays. The results came back this morning. I got cancer in my lung, spine, and brain. I got six months."

"There must be something they can do," Phil said.

"Yeah, they offered a whole arsenal of chemo that will knock me flat. It may kill the cancer, but it will probably kill me first."

"They're doing a lot of great things with chemo these days."

"I've seen what some of my buddies went through with chemo, and cancer took them anyway."

"You can't just give up."

"One thing we learned in combat – when it's your time, it's your time. I got no regrets. I've had a good life, outlived Mary, which she never expected."

"Look, I'm not going to try to talk you into or out of anything. You're old enough to make those choices. But why don't you come with me to the bull riding competition tonight and watch some buckaroos get tossed into the air? It might take your mind off things."

"I believe I'll pass. Why don't you take that little filly of yours instead."

"Who?"

"Annie, the office manager. Don't pretend you don't know what I mean."

"We're just friends."

"Does she know that? 'Cause I see how she lights up whenever I see you together."

"It's a little complicated with her as my employee."

"Where I come from, you don't wait for tomorrow. If you see something you like, you put a ring on it, or you could lose it."

"Good advice," Phil said. "Are you going to be OK here all by yourself?"

"I'm not going to check out if that's what you mean. I made a promise to my buddies back at The Wall."

"Fair enough. I'll bring you back a candy apple."

"You do that."

Phil found Annie in her office putting files away. "C'mon, let's go to the rodeo tonight. I got VIP seats." Annie's face lit up.

"I'd love to – I love the rodeo. I even did barrel racing when I was a kid."

"OK, then. Let's do it. I'll pick you up at 7:00."

In the car, Phil made a confession. "I've never actually been to a live rodeo before."

"Never?"

"I've seen a few on TV, but never in person."

"That's the only way to experience a rodeo – live and up close."

"I think they have a big one in Kissimmee each year, but I've just never gone."

"I've gone to rodeos since I was a kid. Rodeo cowboys were my heroes," Annie said. "Almost married one."

"What happened?"

"He forgot the line in the wedding vow about 'forsaking all others.'"

"Maybe it's just the way they're hard-wired – tame one stallion, then move on to the next."

"That doesn't work for me."

They arrived at the MetraPark and found their way to the rodeo arena. The VIP section was close to the action, restricted to guests of local community leaders. The back of the tickets defined the dress code. Because TV cameras often panned to the VIP section, everyone was expected to look like they belonged at a rodeo – cowboy hats, shirts, and boots. After all, there was a certain image the city had to maintain. Annie saw a popcorn stand and got in line.

"I can't watch a rodeo without popcorn – it's kinda like the movies, and I have to have popcorn at the movies." With popcorn in hand, they found their seats, so close to the bulls they could smell them.

"This is what you call spitting distance," Annie said.

The night featured the best of bull riding, with the rankest, meanest, most disagreeable creatures ever to draw breath – each one about 1,900 pounds of pure evil.

"Now, explain to me again what the point of this is," Phil said.

"Stay on his back for eight seconds, any way you can," Annie said.

"And what do you get?"

"You get points that accumulate through the entire season. Last year the top rider for the season won $500,000."

"Tough way to make a buck," Phil said.

"Yeah, most riders don't make more than $15,000 to $20,000 a year."

"They could make that much slinging hamburgers, without the broken ribs."

"But there's no glory in hamburgers."

"Well, let's see how much glory there is out here tonight."

The field of hopeful buckaroos did not disappoint. Some of the riders came battle ready, wearing a flack jacket and military-grade helmet with a wired face guard.

"Now, I guarantee that one is married," Phil said.

"Probably. Some of these bulls are known as widow makers."

"Cute," Phil said.

Most of the bulls sent their riders sailing through the air, landing in ways not intended for the human body. A few got their hand so tangled up in the bull rope they could not get free of the bull even after being bucked off. Those moments were the most terrifying for the cowboy and the audience. The bull's erratic twists and turns could snap the rider's arm and even kill him. These were the precious seconds when rodeo clowns earned their pay by climbing on the bull's back in the heat of its fitful rage, to dislodge the rider's tangled hand.

"I don't know how much those clowns get paid, but whatever it is, it's not enough," Phil said. "This is just painful to watch."

"Cowboy up," Annie said.

The ride of the night made the evening worth the price of admission, as one seasoned cowpoke took charge of the orneriest bull in what appeared to be a ballet of man and beast. Straight out of the gate, the rider anticipated each move, every buck, each twist and turn, even when the steer went nearly vertical in its desperation to shed its unwelcome passenger. Though flailed like a rag doll, the cowboy maintained his composure and center of gravity, and held his position for the full eight seconds. At the sound of the buzzer he leaped to the ground, triumphantly waving to the crowd with hat in hand. The audience cheered at this demonstration of mastery, and the judges rewarded him with the high score of the night.

"I'm not ready to call it a night," Annie said. "Let's go on some rides." Phil took her to the bright lights and calliope sounds of the carnival midway. He bought two tickets for the Ferris wheel. They climbed into an empty gondola and took their seats. The large wheel slowly moved them into the sky, where it paused to take on new passengers below.

"What a view," Annie said, looking out at the shimmering night lights of Billings.

"Yeah, I'm looking at it," Phil said, as he studied the luminous glow of her face. She looked back to see Phil transfixed on her. Suddenly, the sprawling twinkling lights below lost her interest, as she turned in her seat to give Phil her full attention. He pulled her near and kissed her slow and easy.

"Wow. What was that?" Annie said.

"Just another thing I've never done before – kiss a girl a hundred feet off the ground." Suddenly the carnival midway lost its allure, and they walked quietly to Phil's Suburban. They drove back to Annie's house and parked in the driveway.

"You've never seen the inside of my house before," Annie said.

"No."

"Would you like to?"

"I'd love to." She look him by the hand and led him to the front door, unlocked it, and took him inside. As she turned on a few lights, he scanned the kitchen to the left and the living room to the right. It was a movie museum, with framed posters of *Casablanca*, *How the West Was Won*, *Junior Bonner*, and *All About Eve*. Knick-knacks in the bookshelves included porcelain statues of Rhett But-ler holding Scarlet O'Hara in his embrace, a snow globe of the scary home of Anthony Perkins' mother in *Psycho*, and a large framed picture of Annie with her arm around Dr. McDreamy from *Grey's Anatomy*. A pillow on the sofa featured the embroidered image of Bette Davis. Annie walked over to him with two glasses of wine. She held out one glass for him.

"What do you think?" she asked. Phil smiled.

"I'm detecting a theme here," he said. He took a sip of wine.

"Yeah, a little shrine to my Hollywood days," she said.

"I like it."

"It wasn't all bad. I learned a lot about myself, so it had a purpose."

"What did you learn?"

"I learned what's important and what's not."

"I guess that's worth three years – kinda like the University of Hollywood," Phil said. He looked at his watch. It was 11:15.

"Don't go," Annie said.

"You're sure?" Phil said. She put her glass down and approached him. He set his glass down, knowing what was coming. They kissed with an urgent passion rising from deep within their hungry souls. Then she began unbuttoning his shirt. He lifted his arms to help by unbuttoning his sleeves over his head. She stroked his bare chest, then kissed it. Cowboy up, he thought. This may be the ride of my life.

The next morning he woke up with the sunrise and looked over at the bare sleek back of Annie as she slept, with a small tattooed bronco at the base of her spine. He rubbed it gently for good luck and kissed the back of her neck. She rolled over.

"Good morning, cowboy," she grinned. "Hungry?"

# CHAPTER 32

Sgt. Mike Belvedere, along with Detective Alex Reynolds, from the Chicago Police Department, marched in lock step through the double doors of Darryl Brooks' office suite. Susan, Darryl's secretary, rose to greet them.

"I'm Sergeant Mike Belvedere with the Billings Police, and I believe you've already met Detective Alex Reynolds, with the Chicago Police."

"Yes, I have. How can I help?"

"We're here to see Darryl Brooks," Alex said.

"I'll let him know you're here." She went to her desk and dialed his number. "Mr. Brooks, the police are here again. They want to speak with you...No, they didn't have an appointment...OK, I'll tell them." She set down the receiver and turned to the policemen.

"Mr. Brooks said he's already late for a meeting downtown and regrets he can't speak with you right now. Is there another time..." she said, but could not finish her sentence, because the two policemen walked past her and helped themselves into Darryl's office. He stood behind his desk gathering files beside his open briefcase.

"Mr. Brooks..." Alex began, but Darryl cut him off.

"Did my secretary not make it clear that I'm already late for a meeting?" Alex closed the lid to the briefcase while Mike broke the news.

"You're not going to make that meeting," Mike said.

"And why not?"

"Because you are coming with us down to the police station," Mike said.

"I don't think so," Darryl said.

"You can either come with us voluntarily or we can arrest you and haul you in," Mike said.

"What is it now? I already answered your questions," Darryl said.

"We've got some video to show you and some new questions," Alex said. Darryl turned to Mike.

"And who are you?" Mike produced his badge.

"Detective Mike Belvedere – Billings Police," Mike said.

"So, which way do you want it? Friendly or ugly?" Alex said.

"My attorney said if I'm not under arrest I don't have to answer anything," Darryl said.

"If we have to arrest you, you're not going home today. But if you come voluntarily and we like your answers, you're free to go and we won't bother you again," Alex said. Darryl considered those two options and figured he could talk his way out of just about anything, and as for videos, he couldn't imagine any videos that would spoil his day.

"All right, let's get this witch hunt over with," Darryl said. "I want my lawyer there – where are you taking me?"

"Homan Square," Alex said. Darryl buzzed Susan.

"Yes, Mr. Brooks," Susan said.

"I'm going with these gentlemen to the Homan Square Police Station. Call Lane Borman, my personal attorney, and have him meet us there."

"Yes, sir," Susan said. Darryl hung up the phone.

"All right, can I meet you there?" Darryl said.

"No, you can leave your car here. We'll all go together," Alex said. Darryl pointed to the door.

"Lead the way."

Mid-week, mid-day freeway traffic through Chicago moved

along with few slowdowns, and the three arrived at Homan Square in about twenty minutes. It was large brick five-story structure on the west side of Chicago with numerous interrogation rooms. They ushered Darryl into an empty room with a single table, four chairs, and a two-way mirror.

"As soon as your lawyer gets here, we'll bring him in," Alex said. "Can we get you anything to drink?"

"Maybe some water," Darryl said. Alex left the room. In a few minutes an assistant brought in a small bottled water. Mike and Alex waited in the viewing room, watching Darryl through the two-way mirror.

"Without a corpse, the most we could get Darryl on is lying to the police about his whereabouts," Alex said. "We need a body."

"We'll see how much he is willing to spill," Mike said.

"I've got to make a few calls. Let me know when his lawyer gets here," Alex said. Mike nodded. In about twenty minutes a uniformed cop ushered Lane Borman to Darryl's interview room. Mike stopped him at the door.

"You're Mr. Brooks' counsel?" Mike asked. Lane shook hands.

"Yes, I'm Lane Borman. Now, what's this all about?"

"We've got an unsolved murder in Billings, Montana. We've got some questions to ask your client, and some video tape for him to watch and help us understand," Alex said.

"Is he a suspect?" Lane asked.

"Definitely a person of interest," Mike said. Now that Lane understood the gravity of this interview, he was curious to see what kind of cards everybody held. The three entered the interview room. Mike carried a laptop computer under his arm. He set it down, then produced a recorder pen and set it beside the laptop. Mike took the lead in this round of questioning. He set down the transcript from the initial interview held a few days earlier with Alex and Ray.

"Darryl, I read over the answers you gave in the first interview with Detectives Reynolds and Clemons," Mike said. Lane turned to Darryl.

"You've talked to these men already?"

"They had some questions the other day about a missing person," Darryl said.

"Well, let me go on the record saying that whatever answers he gave to your earlier questions were without benefit of counsel," Lane said.

"Noted," Mike said. He turned to Darryl. "The other day you were asked the last time you spoke to Walter Angler, and you said it was at his retirement party last February." He lifted the recorder pen and set it in front of Darryl. "We have a recorded conversation that Walter Angler made between you and him in June. Listen." He pushed the PLAY button.

> *What do you think?*
> *I don't like it. She could put us all in jail.*
> *What do we do?*
> *We have to make sure she doesn't talk. Ever.*

"That is your voice and Walter's voice. We had it verified by someone who knows both of you. What were you talking about? Who is 'she' that could put both of you in jail?"

"I'm going to advise my client not to answer that on the grounds of self-incrimination," Lane said. Mike moved on.

"When you said 'We have to make sure she doesn't talk. Ever' – talk about what?" Again Lane interrupted.

"Once again, I'm going to advise my client not to answer that question." Undaunted, Mike continued.

"You said the last time you saw Walter Angler was at his retirement party last February, is that correct?" Darryl did not know if he should deny or agree with his earlier statement. He looked at Lane for rescue.

"That's OK – you don't have to say it again," Mike said. "We've already got it on the record. Unless you want to change your answer. But before you do, you might want to look at this." He flipped open his laptop computer and pressed the PLAY button. The screen came alive and displayed the surveillance footage from the Rimrock Mall security camera on July 24. It showed Walter parking his Lincoln Continental.

"Now, look at the time stamp on this footage – it says July 24. Now, isn't that Walter's car that just pulled up in the Rimrock Mall?" Mike said. Darryl dared not speak. Lane looked on in dismay. The footage continued to show a Pontiac Grand Prix pull up beside Walter's car.

Just then, an officer opened the door and interrupted the interview.

"I'm looking for Mike Belvedere."

"That's me," Mike said.

"Your partner is holding on line 2. He said it's urgent."

"Could you tell him I'll call him back?"

"He said you are going to want to hear what he has to say."

"All right. Where can I take it?"

"You can use my desk. It's right outside," the officer said. Mike turned to Alex.

"Excuse me for a minute."

Mike picked up the phone at the officer's desk and punched line 2.

"This is Mike."

"You're not going to believe this, but they found a body a few weeks ago about five miles west of Lemmon, South Dakota. It's been on ice at the local hospital. Two slugs in the chest. They were trying to ID it with no luck. Then they remembered our wire. They sent us a photo of the face, and Mrs. Angler ID'd him. It's Walter."

"Ballistics?" Mike said.

"The slugs are from a Glock 43."

"What a stroke of luck."

"That's not all. The Lemmon Police got a call from a driver who stopped by the side of the road and ID'd the car that dumped the body."

"This just gets better and better," Mike said. "I got to get back to the interview, but see if you can find out if Darryl is registered for a Glock 43. If he is, then get a warrant for us to search his house."

"I'm on it," Earl said. Mike returned to the interview room.

"Now, where were we? Oh, yes, the Pontiac. Now, that Pontiac Grand Prix – isn't that your car?" Darryl said nothing. "We know it is – we've already checked the license plate and registration. But you told the Chicago detectives that you were home all day on July 24. So, how does your car end up in Billings while you're home? Was it stolen? No, I don't think so, or you would have reported it. Borrowed? If so, tell us who borrowed it so we can talk to him and clear this up. The truth is that you drove your car to Billings, didn't you?"

"Don't answer that," Lane said. Then they watched the laptop recording as Walter stepped out of his car and looked directly into the surveillance camera, then climbed into the passenger seat of the Pontiac.

"Now, here we have Walter – clearly Walter – getting into your Pontiac. Now, watch what happens in a few minutes." He fast forwarded the tape two minutes. "Now, look at this." They all watched as two muzzle flashes reflected off the dashboard windshield, then someone covered Walter up with a blanket. "Those look like two gunshots, what do you think?" Mike asked. "Did you shoot Walter Angler?" He quickly turned to Darryl's lawyer. "But, how could he have?" Then he turned back to Darryl.

"It couldn't have been you, because you said to Detective Reynolds here that you were home in Chicago all day long on July 24, isn't that right? And you can't be in two places at once." Darryl knew the hammer was about to drop. He didn't know how – he didn't know what, but he knew he was about to be shown the gates of hell.

"The truth is, you drove all the way to Billings from July 23 to 24 to meet with Walter, but you were getting low on gas. So, you stopped at Casey's Corner Convenience Store at Five Points, just five miles north of Billings, to fill up. But because you paid cash, you had to go inside the store to pay for it. What you didn't stop to realize is that the store had a security camera mounted behind the cash register in case of robberies. And look who got caught on film." Mike pushed the PLAY button and the tape showed Darryl stepping up to the cash register, plain as day. "And look at the time stamp," Mike said. It read "July 24, 4:00 p.m." Lane could only sit back and groan.

"Just one more thing – we have the body, two slugs in the chest from a Glock 43. You don't happen to own a Glock 43, do you?" Mike said to Darryl. Darryl could not speak. Alex spoke next.

"We have a warrant to search your car for blood splatter and to search your house for weapons. Until those jobs are completed, you will be held here in detention." An officer led Darryl to a holding cell. In the hallway, Lane spoke to Mike.

"Is my client being charged?" Lane asked.

"Not yet. But the walls are closing in. He is being held, pending the results of our crime scene investigators and a house search for the Glock. We'll let you know what we find."

Traces of blood were recovered from the floor carpet fibers of the passenger side of Darryl's Pontiac. The blood type matched Walter Angler's A Positive type. The house search uncovered a Glock 43 in Darryl's wall safe. A subsequent ballistics test matched the slugs taken from Walter's body to Darryl's Glock. Checkmate.

Darryl Brooks was charged with first degree murder and extradited to Billings for trial. After three days of testimony and the presentation of evidence, the jury came back with a unanimous verdict of guilty. From her seat in the gallery, Clara Angler wept tears of relief, knowing that her husband's killer would be punished and that she could finally give Walter a proper burial. Sylvia

Longwood's family, as well as the Ramsey family, sat through the entire trial and felt a sense of closure that the two men who bore the blame for the loss of their loved ones were brought to justice.

Outside the courtroom, Mrs. Ramsey's son, Dale, took Phil aside.

"I got no beef with the facility. I just want you to know that I appreciate all you did to hold these men accountable. My mother can rest easy now. We're not going to bring any lawsuits against The Sanctuary. My mother loved that place, and I know it's in good hands now. So, I'll leave you in peace."

Darlene Longwood, Sylvia's sister, stepped up next and gave Phil a hug.

"Thank you for clearing my sister's name. She was smart to choose you to make things right," she said.

"Thank you for trusting me with those incident reports. They made all the difference," Phil said. He noticed Mike Belvedere leaving the courtroom and cornered him.

"You deserve all the credit for this verdict," Phil said. "I don't know how you did it, but I wouldn't want your job." Mike gave him a wink and a handshake.

"The truth is, I wouldn't want your job," Mike said.

The Chairman of United Senior Living, Leland Thompson, attended the trial at the request of both opposing counsels, in case they required his testimony, which ultimately was not needed. He approached Phil outside the courthouse steps.

"Nasty bit of business," Leland said. "I know you've worked your heart out to make The Sanctuary a profit center, and I have no doubt this unfortunate turn of events will be a set-back."

"I choose to look at this as a vindication, and that's always good," Phil said.

"This is probably an awkward time to bring it up, but we seem to have an opening in the Director of Operations slot, and I wouldn't blame you if you walked away from this mess. I guess what I'm saying is, the job is yours if you want it. Don't you worry about The Sanctuary. We'll find someone qualified to dig this project out of the ditch."

"I'm flattered at the offer, but I'm not one to cut and run when things get rough. If you don't mind, I'd like to stay and see this thing through before I consider any other offers." Leland shook his hand.

"I like your style. Stay in touch. If you need anything, let me know."

# CHAPTER 33

At the end of workday on Monday, Annie sat down with Phil in his office.

"I've got something to tell you," Annie said. "I was holding it in over the weekend, 'cause I didn't want to spoil anything from the other night, after the rodeo. But now is as good a time as any." Phil cleared his desk and gave her his full attention.

"OK – I'm listening," he said.

"Last week I got a call from my Hollywood agent."

"Oh?"

"He wanted to let me know that I'm being considered for a leading role in a new TV series for FX that's in development right now. It's going to be a modern western that's kinda playing off the popularity of westerns making the rounds on cable. They're looking for a fresh face, not someone who's already been in a series. They've auditioned several actresses to play the wife of a country doctor, but none of them know how to ride a horse convincingly or shoot a rifle. And you just can't leave that stuff up to stunt doubles when you want to do close-ups. Anyway, he's set up a screen test for me this week, to try out for the part, but he thinks it's mine for the asking." Phil tried to catch his breath from the punch to his gut and the stab to his heart. He cleared his throat.

"Is that what you want?" Phil said.

"Yeah, I'd be crazy to turn it down."

"Does that mean you gotta move back to LA?" Annie held her breath for a beat.

"Yeah, it kinda does."

"For how long?"

"Well, we gotta film a pilot, and the network has to approve it. If they like it, they'll order another twenty episodes, then we'll see what happens. But if it's a hit, I'll be obligated for at least five seasons."

"OK – I get it. So, this is good bye?" Phil said.

"Do you want me to turn it down? Do you want me to stay here?"

"No – I don't want to be your mother that you resent for killing your dream. If you choose to stay here, it has to be because that's what you want."

Annie searched her feelings and knew that she let her barriers down and allowed herself to fall in love with Phil. She knew it when she invited him to her house and felt ready for the likely chance that the evening would end in bed. When he spent the night, she took it as his reciprocal expression of love. Now those attachment chemicals surged through her body, despite the fact that neither of them had ever actually uttered the words "I love you," the surest journey to a broken heart. But now was no time for games. Phil deserved to know the emotional stakes at risk.

"I'm scared," she said. "I think I'm in love with you, and I can't stand the thought of leaving just when we're connecting. But this might be my only chance to make it in Hollywood."

"If it makes any difference, I know I'm in love with you. I haven't felt this way in fifteen years."

"Then, tell me to stay," Annie said. Phil shook his head.

"No, you gotta follow your dream wherever it takes you. I'm not going to guilt you into staying. If we are meant to be, it'll happen. So, go. I'll find someone to fill your shoes in the office. It'll be a tall order, but you know what they say – the cemetery is full of indispensable people." He got up and held out his arms for a good-bye hug. Annie stood up, as tears welled up. They embraced for a long moment.

"Why does this hurt so much?" she whispered as she rested her head on his shoulder.

"Love is kinda nutty about the whole good-bye thing." They kissed – not like any other kiss they had ever tasted before. It was sad and painful. Not the kind of kiss you would try to prolong. Annie slowly pulled away and walked out the door. She turned briefly and blew Phil one last kiss. The next day she caught the first flight to LA.

Phil counted on the Senior Fair to pull his chestnuts out of the fire. It was a gamble, to be sure, but he knew positive publicity could rescue the facility from doom. With the fair only one week away, advertisements targeted the Billings and Bozeman newspapers, bolstered by radio spots and TV announcements. Residents and families felt surging pride that The Sanctuary might bask in some flattering press for a change. In preparation, flags, banners, and pennants festooned the campus. Directional signs and parking attendants assured that visitor traffic would be orderly and free of log jams.

A giant classic and collectible car rally kicked off the exciting three-day event, the first weekend of September. Several local car clubs reserved large sections of the front parking lot to showcase their rare and coveted vehicles, including the Billings Classic Car Club, the Yellowstone Roaring 20s Auto Club, the Montana Car Club, the Montana Thunderbird Club, the Moonshine Car Club, and CMYRYD. Phil strolled the parking lot and introduced himself to each of the participants.

"Now, I can understand the names of every other club except yours," Phil said to Jasper Donovan, president of CMYRYD. "How do you pronounce the name of your club?"

"Easy," Jasper said. "Once I explain it, you'll never forget it. It's simply three words compressed together. The first letter is also a word – 'C'. The next two letters combine to make the second word – 'MY'. And the last three letters make the final word, pronounced just the way it looks – 'RYD'. Put them together and what have you got?" Phil had to think about it for a moment, then he got it and smiled broadly.

"See My Ride," Phil pronounced.

"Exactly," Jasper said.

"Pretty clever," Phil said.

The parking lot soon filled with classic Mustangs, hot rods, muscle cars, Euro cars, Corvettes, Chevy Camaros, T-Birds, and antiques. Some of the rare and eye-popping cars included a 1932 Bentley, a 1903 Oldsmobile Runabout, a 1908 Ford Model T, a 1932 Packard, a 1933 Pierce-Arrow, and a 1939 Cadillac La Salle. One proud owner of a 1915 Ford Model T Roadster paid for his trip to Billings by offering anyone a ride around the parking lot for $5.00. The line for his unique attraction stretched almost to the street.

When the gates opened at 9:00 a.m., a crowd of 500 eager guests poured into the massive outdoor exhibit, a virtual museum of American automobile history. Parents and grandparents felt transported to their own childhood, recalling cars they grew up with or were driven by their grandparents. Facility residents gravitated to cars that reminded them of those glorious "days gone by," when license plates had only three letters, cars had only two gears – forward and backward – tires were supported by wooden-spoked wheel rims, and rumble seats, which some allege were designed to keep mothers-in-law at a suitable distance from the driver.

Cars of similar make and model clustered together. Owners of the classic 1956 T-Birds found their simpaticos and assembled in a covey to swap stories of the joys and pains of car restoration. Muscle cars drew legions of admirers. Grandmothers quietly remembered the car where they received their first kiss and rode to the senior prom. Grandpas grinned at the memory of Sunday afternoons under the hood, tinkering with such classics as the 1969

Dodge Charger, the 1966 Shelby GT350, and the 1964 Pontiac GTO, when a real man was measured in cubic inches, carburetors, and horsepower.

Noontime food vendors lined the perimeter of the parking lot, providing taste treats for every palate, from hot dogs to steak-on-a-stick, thick crust pizza, burritos, and all things barbeque. Picnic tables with sun-protecting umbrellas gave patrons a welcome rest to refuel, jabber, gossip, and gabble.

Families with loved ones who called The Sanctuary their home proudly invited friends to take a look inside and see how good life could be for seniors. Folks who thought they knew what a retirement community was were pleasantly shocked at the endless amenities available for residents.

"I had no idea this place had a swimming pool and shuffleboard courts," one visitor admitted. "My mother would love this." Another visitor gushed, "Dad should see their woodworking shop here. They've got tools he only wishes he had." By the afternoon, designated resident hosts logged in over fifty tours and rented three vacant units.

By the end of the day six classic cars changed owners, strangers became new best friends, and The Sanctuary suddenly found new life. After the last classic car rumbled out of the parking lot, Phil made the rounds inside, thanking each department and every resident host for their contribution in making the day a success. In the lobby Tina helped log into the computer every visitor who signed the guest book for follow-up thank-you notes and invitations for a free guest meal to "Taste and See that This Is the Place to Be."

"Are we done for the night?" Tina asked Phil. He looked around the lobby and sighed.

"If we're not, it'll just have to keep till tomorrow," Phil said.

The next morning delivery trucks from local department stores lined up outside the facility to drop off their finest women's apparel for the fashion show. After breakfast the dining room underwent a transformation to resemble a fashion show runway. Tables were pushed back and three rows of chairs framed the glitzy runway, where thirty of the facility's ladies agreed to model the latest in fashion for family, friends, the curious public, and the local media. No restrictions were placed on prospective models. The event organizers encouraged residents regardless of age, height, weight, or mobility. Three of the designated models were wheelchair-bound, accompanied by their sons or daughters, who pushed them from behind while they waved at the adoring crowds.

The show began at 10:00 a.m. with the latest in casual wear for the summer. Musical fanfare signaled the ladies to strut their stuff, starting with Mrs. Walsh. She stepped onto the stage and strutted as bold as you please with sunglasses and a wide-brim summer hat. She sported deep-pocketed linen pants, available in light grey, blue, and green, along with a shirt collar solid casual blouse with rolled-up long sleeves, and sandals. Her necklace featured a delicate gold chain with seashell baubles. Over her shoulder she rocked a basket-weave tote, as though she were headed for the park to read the latest romance novel. The audience cheered at her sassy attitude as she paused at the end of the runway, struck a pose, then sashayed back.

Evening wear featured some lovely gowns worn by a few of the silver-haired fashion mavens of The Sanctuary. But the high point belonged to Evelyn Cole. Wheelchair-bound, her grandson pushed her to center stage, where she stopped and, with the steady hand of her escort, rose from her chair and turned full circle to showcase a lovely travel ensemble. The audience rewarded her dash and verve with a round of applause.

At the municipal golf course father-son teams lined up for their last-minute instructions.

"As you know, this event was limited to any of the gents who live at The Sanctuary, and the son of their choosing, to create a father-son team competition, with a $1,000 first place prize going to the two-man team posting the lowest combined score," Phil said. "We have twenty courageous teams competing here today, so we divided you up into five foursomes. Standard rules of golf apply. The skies are clear, the course is dry, and the mood is friendly. So, be safe, have a great day, and we'll see you all back at the clubhouse."

The favorite to win this cordial tournament was Doug Nash and his son Gary, both lifelong students of the game. Doug retired from his executive position at Eagle Oil Corporation ten years earlier at age sixty-seven. Three years ago he and his wife moved into a two-bedroom deluxe at The Sanctuary, and Doug tricked out his own golf cart to look like a Rolls Royce from the front end. Now at seventy-seven, he still drove 240 yards off the tee and boasted a 6 handicap. His son Gary, a local dentist, managed to get in at least three rounds a week. Neither of them needed the prize money, but bragging rights at the next Rotary meeting made the challenge enticing.

This was, regrettably, not a good day for Doug. His game ran off the rails when he scored a 16 on the par-4 ninth hole. The score included an unplayable lie from the tee, a two-stroke penalty after the ball ricocheted off a tree and struck him, and five consecutive strokes from the woods. After he and his son good-naturedly endured the endless razzing from the other players, he returned to the fateful ninth hole, where he stripped off his golf shirt and hung it on the cup's flag as a "sacrifice" to the golf gods.

Just before dinner, the golfers returned with tales of the agonies and ecstasies of the day. The first prize went to Frank Halsted, apartment 233, and his son Bruce, who turned in a combined score of 162. Phil presented them with the $1,000 check and ended the night with the "sand trap" award going to the unlucky Nash team.

Prospect tours for the day totaled forty-five, with another four apartments reserved. That put the facility over ninety-two percent occupancy, a feather in any facility's cap.

"This is fantastic," Phil told Tina at the end of the day. "This is just what we needed."

"Two days down – one more to go," she said.

# CHAPTER 34

The Fall Festival capped off the final day with two events. First, the morning offered a chance for residents to show off their cooking skills with a fruit pie contest. Residents were challenged to create a fresh fruit pie of their choosing, to be judged by five high-profile dignitaries ready to sample the best of Billings' pastry artisans. Judges included the Governor of the State, the Mayor of Billings, the U.S. House Representative for Montana, the Billings Chief of Police, and the President of the Billings Chamber of Commerce. Pies would be scored according to several categories, including appearance, consistency, flavor, and texture. First, second, and third place winners each received gift cards, worth $500, $250, and $100 respectively, to Albertson's Grocery Store, which sponsored the event. Resident contestants were allowed to use their own personal apartment kitchen to create their masterpiece, with ingredients purchased from any local grocery store in Billings. To be sure that contestants did not sneak in a professionally prepared pie from some offsite mystery chef, roving referees would make unannounced inspections of the progress of each creation.

The event attracted twenty-seven residents to answer the challenge, and all met in the central dining room at 9:00 a.m. to review the rules.

"You will have until 2:00 p.m. to create your pie and deliver it here to the judging area," Phil said. "You can have a partner to help, but it has to be created in your own apartment kitchen." The judges were introduced to everyone, a pretty splashy lineup of dignitaries, and the contestants got to work.

The second event of the day was an arts and crafts challenge designed to showcase the artistic flair of the facility's residents. Contestants were invited to submit a sample of their artistic achievements for consideration in the competition. The first, second, and third place winners would receive $500, $250, and $100 respectively, the same as the pastry competition. At the start of the day residents submitted samples of their pottery masterpieces, woodworking achievements, quilting, flower arrangements, jewelry, and paintings. One gentleman created a ship in a bottle, another submitted a scale model of the Eiffel Tower from toothpicks, and another offered his collectible hand-carved and painted wooden ducks.

Phil remembered Tom Reese's lovely acrylic painting of his wife hanging in his apartment.

"You should enter that painting in the competition. You could win," Phil said to Tom.

"Are you sure? I don't think it would win a prize," Tom said.

"Just enter it. What have you got to lose?" Phil said. Tom reluctantly agreed and set up his painting on an easel in the Arts and Crafts Hall, where the entries were on display.

At the 2:00 deadline the freshly baked pies sat in a long line for judges to sample. Contestants created pies from their old family recipes – apple pies, cherry pies, strawberry pies, raisin pies, blueberry pies, mixed berry pies, plum pies, lemon meringue pies, rhubarb pies, huckleberry pies, cherry-pear pies, banana cream pies, and key lime pies. The mixture of flavors delighted the judges and made their decision nearly impossible. By a close margin, Mrs. Barlow's key lime pie took first place, followed by Mrs. Elwood's mixed berry pie, and finally, Mrs. Fisher's amazing triple berry pie.

The same judges moved to the arts and crafts competition, where entries drew wide praise from spectators and officials alike.

After much debate, the judges submitted their top three picks. Capturing the third place trophy was Charlie Osgood's twenty by twenty-one by six-inch scale wooden model of a 1930 racing schooner, finely and authentically crafted to one-tenth scale. The second place winner was a hand-woven Navajo blanket, fifty-four by thirty-seven inches with indigo blue stripes and white and brown natural churro wool. Finally, the first place prize went to Tom Reese's stunning portrait painting "Leora," with its warm color combinations reminiscent of the seventeenth-century Baroque style of Rembrandt and other Dutch masters.

All winning contestants gathered for a picture that would appear in the *Billings Gazette* the next day. The pastry ladies lined up with their winning pies in hand for a photo, and the judges lined up behind them. Then the three arts and crafts winners stood together for their photo. Tom modestly requested to skip the photo shoot, doggedly holding to his policy of never being photographed in public. The Mayor of Billings insisted that Tom, the first place winner, sit with the others or spoil the ebullience of the entire event. Tom grudgingly agreed, but donned sunglasses and a trilby fedora hat to cover his identity as much as possible.

The article in the newspaper announced the winners of both competitions, and even identified the name of Tom's winning entry – "Leora." When the paper hit the newsstands an alarm rang in Mr. Diamond's computer center. He clicked on the Billings article with the painting entitled "Leora," then studied the photo of the winning artist – Tom Reese. He printed an enlargement of Tom's face and ran it through his facial mapping software. Even with sunglasses and hat for a disguise, the nose, cheeks, and jawline of Tom gave him away, and the software reported with ninety-two percent certainty that this was the face of Vincent Wallace. The next day Mr. Diamond met with Johnny Giovani and handed him an envelope.

"Here's your man. He's living under the alias 'Tom Reese' in a Billings, Montana, retirement community called The Sanctuary." Johnny's face slowly twisted into a sinister self-satisfied smile.

"Son of a bitch," he mumbled. He pushed a button on his office phone.

"Bring in the envelope," he said to the other end. "How did you track him down?"

"Facial recognition software," Mr. Diamond said. "It won't be long before nobody can hide."

The secretary came into the office with the envelope and handed it to Johnny, who in turn handed it to Mr. Diamond.

"I believe this concludes our arrangement," Johnny said. Mr. Diamond glanced at the contents of the envelope, a check for two million dollars. He smiled and extended his hand.

"I appreciate doing business with you." And with that Mr. Diamond turned and left. Johnny got on the phone.

"Marco, this is Johnny. We found Vincent...Billings, Montana...We'll need someone to meet us at the airport with the necessary artillery...tomorrow...Isn't Griff out of Salt Lake City...He'll do just fine."

# CHAPTER 35

Johnny and Marco landed in the Billings Airport in early afternoon and waited on a bench outside baggage claim for Griff to pick them up. A black Chevy Tahoe with Utah plates pulled up to the curb, and a lean man with a trim beard got out.

"Need a ride into town?" Griff asked. Since neither Johnny nor Marco had ever met Griff before, they requested some verification.

"You got some ID?" said Johnny. Griff pulled out his wallet and handed over his Utah driver's license. Johnny matched the photo with Griff's face, then handed it back.

"Just crossing our T's," Johnny said. Griff pointed to the Tahoe.

"Climb aboard. I think I got everything you asked for," Griff said. Inside the car, Griff handed each passenger a gun case. They opened them up to find a 9mm Glock 43 with noise suppressor and two twenty-one-round clips. They smiled at the hardware.

"Just so I'm clear – it's gonna take all three of us to exterminate one old man eking out his final days in a nursing home? I don't get it," Griff said.

"In the first place, it's a retirement community – not a nursing home," Johnny said.

"Oh, I see – that's why we need all three of us?" Griff said.

"Marco and I are coming along, not because we don't think you can handle it, but we want to personally look into that shitbag's face as we put a bullet through his brain pan," Johnny said.

"OK, fair enough," Griff said. "Let's get to it." They drove into town and parked across the street from the Billings Florist Shop. They waited for two hours until the company's delivery truck pulled into the florist parking lot and the driver went inside. The death squad exited the black Tahoe and followed the delivery driver in the front door.

"Is that it for the day?" the driver asked the receptionist.

"That's the last delivery. Thanks, Brian," she said. The driver dropped the keys on the counter and headed to the back room to change out of his uniform coveralls with the company name and logo stitched onto the front and back. Marco followed him into the back room.

"Hey, you can't go back there," the receptionist called out to Marco. He ignored her, as Johnny grabbed the keys to the delivery truck off the counter. The receptionist suddenly felt outnumbered.

"Wait a minute. That's not yours," she protested loudly. "What do you think you're doing?" Griff pulled out his 9mm Glock and put two slugs into the receptionist – chest and head.

"I didn't need to hear anymore of that," Griff said. Johnny went to the store windows and closed the blinds while Griff went to the refrigerated display case and took out the largest bouquet he could find, then grabbed a gift card from the front counter. Marco returned to the lobby now wearing the Florist Shop coveralls no longer needed by the ill-fated driver, now a lifeless body lying beside the buckets of flowers back in the cooler. Johnny flipped the CLOSED sign into full view. The three walked out of the store and climbed into the company delivery truck.

At The Sanctuary, Tina looked at the clock – 7:30 p.m. – time to close up the reception desk. A few pockets of residents lingered in the dining room, comparing notes on their favorite TV shows. Allan Dodge, head of Security, stepped out of the security screening room and locked the door.

"I'm going to see if there's any leftover Chicken Coq Au Vin from dinner," Allan said.

"I gotta get home. My boyfriend's taking me out tonight," Tina said. Allan disappeared into the dining room just as the Billings Florist delivery truck pulled up to the front door. Marco, dressed as the delivery driver, entered the lobby with an impressive bouquet in hand and a bulge in his coveralls around his waist from the Glock tucked into his waist band.

"I've got a delivery for Tom Reese, but I don't have his apartment number," Marco said, handing Tina the incomplete gift card. It read, "Congratulations on your first-place prize in the painting competition at the Fall Festival, from Big Horn Art Gallery, to Tom Reese, Apt. ___."

"You can see they left the apartment number empty. I just need his number so I can get this delivered," Marco said. Suddenly every alarm bell in Tina's brain began to ring like a five-alarm fire, but she managed to keep a cool head.

"Well, we're not allowed to give out residents' apartment numbers, but if you'll leave the flowers here, I'll see that he gets it," Tina said.

"Well, you see, they paid extra to make sure we hand-delivered it," Marco said. "Could you just make an exception this one time?" Tina thought for a moment.

"I suppose," Tina said. "He's in 350." Marco gave her a wink.

"You know, on second thought, I'll just leave the flowers here so you don't get in trouble. Thanks. You've been very helpful." Marco gave her a smile, turned, and left. Tina flew into action. She grabbed the phone and called Phil, who was already upstairs in his apartment.

"Mr. Branson," she said at a level just below panic. "Someone down here just asked for Tom Reese's apartment number." Phil jumped to his feet. Oh, my god, he thought.

"Did you recognize him?"

"No, but he was from the Billings Florist Shop with a big bouquet."

"What did you tell him?"

"I hemmed and hawed for a minute, then I told him 350."

"Then what did he do?"

"He just turned and left."

"Where is he now?" Tina peered at the front door, where the truck just pulled away.

"He just left. What do you want me to do?"

"Is Allan still in his office?"

"No, he just went to the dining room looking for leftovers."

"Go find him – tell him to meet me in his security screening room, then call 911 and tell them that armed men are trying to get into the building, then get the hell out of there."

"Yes, sir, Mr. Branson." She hung up and called 911.

"911 – what's your emergency?"

"This is The Sanctuary Retirement Community. There are armed men trying to get into the building. Somebody needs to get here fast."

"I'll send a patrol car right over. Is there some place safe you can get to?"

"Yes, I think so," Tina said.

"Then go there now."

Tina had other things to do first. She ran to the dining room in search of Allan. Phil grabbed his coat and ran out of his apartment for the stairwell.

Marco climbed into the delivery truck and turned to the others.

"Easy peazy. He's in 350," he said.

"OK," Johnny said. "Let's drive this truck out of sight. Then we get into the building from a side door and take a little elevator ride to the third floor." Marco drove the truck to the west side of the building, where they parked and got out, guns in hand. Griff brought along a large crowbar just in case the side doors were locked. Amazingly, the first side door they tried was open. Johnny stuck his head in to see if the hallway was empty – it was. They eased inside, with weapons tucked inside their coats, and found the elevator landing, climbed aboard, and pushed "3."

Just as the elevator cabin moved upward, Phil met Allan in the screening room.

"It's judgment day – we've got intruders in the building. I need you to find them." He pointed to the wall of security screens. They both scanned the screens by rows and columns until they saw the assassins on the third floor elevator landing, checking the room numbering plaque and turning to the right. They watched the screen as the security camera at the end of the hallway broadcast the killers' every move. They pulled out their weapons and checked their clips.

"Holy shit," Allan said. "What do they want?"

"They want Tom Reese, but I don't have time to explain. Can you shut the elevator down from here?"

"Yeah – why?" Allan said.

"These hoods are looking for apartment 350. In about a minute they are going to discover there is no such number. That's when all hell's going to break loose. When they get back in the elevator and close the door, lock it down so they can't get out."

"OK, but they can get out through the trap door in the ceiling," Allan said.

"I know, we just need to slow them down till the cavalry gets here." Phil turned to leave.

"Where you going?" Allan asked.

"I gotta get Tom out of the building, and I got to get some back-up." He grabbed a walkie-talkie off the table and tossed its companion to Allan. "Let me know when they get to the bottom floor again." Before Allan could ask what Phil meant by "backup", Phil was already out the door. His first stop was Tom's apartment 185. He raced down the hallway and pounded on Tom's door.

"Who is it?" Tom called back as he went to see who was there. He opened his door to see Phil in a state of panic.

"They found you – you understand what I'm saying? They are in the building right now – three of them with guns."

"Where are they?" Tom asked.

"They're on the third floor right now, but they're coming down. You gotta get out of here. Follow the plan – head for the woods behind the building. I gotta make a stop first, but then I'll be right behind you, and the police are on the way." Tom grabbed his coat and reached into the duffel bag that always sat by the front door. He pulled out his pocket pistol and ran for the end of the hallway, where the door led to the pool deck and the back woods.

As predicted, the assassins found the numbers at the end of the hallway only went up to 348.

"What the hell?" Griff said. They began back-tracking to the elevator when a contract therapist stepped into the hallway from a resident's apartment. They quickly slipped their guns inside their coats.

"Excuse me, Ma'am," Griff said. "We're looking for 350, but we're not finding it."

"That's 'cause there is no 350," the therapist said.

"Well, maybe we got it wrong. We're looking for Tom Reese. Would you know what apartment he's in?"

"I don't know. I don't really work here – I'm just a contract therapist. You can ask down at the front desk." She smiled and passed them by on her way to the staircase. Once she was out of earshot, Griff turned to the others.

"We've been had," Griff said. "We gotta get to that reception desk and find the resident roster." They jumped back into the elevator and pushed LOBBY. The door closed and the cabin made it about halfway between the floors when Allan pushed the ELEVATOR STOP button, and the cabin jerked to a sudden halt. He watched from the surveillance camera in the cabin as the trio refused to be trapped for long. They hoisted each other up and out of the cabin through the escape hatch in the ceiling and found a ladder along the side of the elevator shaft to shinny down to the main floor.

Phil made a quick stop at 115 – Joe Henjum's apartment. No time for courtesies – he didn't even bother to knock. He used his master key to bolt through the front door. Joe had just finished dinner and sat in his lounger enjoying a night cap. Phil's sudden intrusion stunned him.

"Joe, I'm sorry for the intrusion, but I need your M18 right now," he said as he raced to the gun rack.

"What happened? Have the Russians landed?" Joe asked. Phil fumbled around with the box of cartridges.

"Worse – three hitmen are in the building right now. They're here to kill Tom Reese, down in 185." He tucked the M18 in his belt and stuck a handful of bullets in his pants pockets. Joe stood up.

"Why?" Joe asked.

"No time to explain," Phil said.

"Where's Tom now?" Joe asked.

"He's already out back in the woods with a pistol of his own. I gotta lure these killers out of the building so nobody in here gets hurt. But I don't know what to do once we're are all out there in the open." Joe reached over and grabbed his 1911 .45 automatic.

"I know what to do," Joe said as he checked the clip of his .45. "Jungle fighting Vietnam style. That's what I'm trained for."

"Hell no – you're not coming with me," Phil said.

"You haven't got a chance against three professionals, so shut up and get moving." Phil saw a side of Joe he'd never seen before, barking orders in full Marine take-charge mode. Joe slid his clip into the base of the grip, pulled the slide back to load a cartridge into the chamber, and shoved Phil out the door.

"C'mon – let's go," Joe said, as he shut the door behind him. The two moved down the hallway.

"OK – what do we do?" Phil asked.

"The VC were champions at luring us into ambushes. It was always fire, turn, and run to suck us in. We gotta take a page out of their playbook."

# CHAPTER 36

Phil got on his walkie-talkie.

"Allan, come in. This is Phil. Where are they?" The walkie-talkie squawked back.

"They just walked out of the elevator shaft door and they're heading for the lobby. What do you want me to do?"

"Just get the hell out of there," Phil said. Phil knew which hallway offered a straight shot view from the exit door to the front desk. He turned to Joe.

"Come with me," Phil said. He led Joe to the south side of the building where the front desk had a clean view all the way down one hallway to the patio exit door.

"OK – I'm going to lure them out. Just be ready when they come through this door." Phil opened the hallway exit door and motioned for Joe to get outside. Joe stepped out and looked for a fox hole, but settled for a cluster of pool chairs heaped together. He hid behind his own little home-made parapet, pistol at the ready, and waited. Inside, Phil stood beside the commercial exit door, his hand leaning on the panic cross-bar, his heart pounding. In a moment he saw the three gunmen at the other end of the hall, rummaging around the reception desk.

"If you're looking for Vincent Wallace, he's out here," Phil shouted. They turned in the direction of Phil's voice, spotted him, and ran towards him. Phil immediately bolted through the exit door, looking for Joe.

"I'm over here," Joe called out. "Now, get down." Phil looked for cover in the twilight of the evening, as the exit door burst open and Griff boldly stepped out, followed by Marco. Phil spun around and got off a panicked shot that drew attention, giving Joe a clear shot at Griff. He planted a slug dead center and Griff sank to the ground in stunned disbelief, then fell forward dead. Marco returned fire and hit Joe in the torso, knocking him over. Phil got off four more rounds, undisciplined and wild. One bullet hit the exit door, another hit the building, a third ricocheted off the concrete deck, and a random slug hit Marco in the leg. He fell to the ground clutching his wound, trying to stem the hemorrhaging. That gave Phil time to check on Joe, whose body lay motionless on the deck. Johnny lunged from the exit door into a clump of shrubbery nearby. Phil crawled away from Joe to a barbeque grill and hid behind it while he frantically refilled his clip, then slid the clip back into place. Johnny called out to his partners in crime.

"Griff – you OK?" No answer. Phil scanned over to see Griff's lifeless body, face down on the deck. "Marco?" Johnny called out next. Marco called back in a trembling voice.

"I been shot. I can't move." Phil took that opportunity to crawl deeper into the recesses of the patio.

"Tom," Phil shouted in a loud whisper.

"I'm over here," Tom called back, pistol in hand, positioned behind a nearby tree at the edge of the woods. Phil dodged his way through the shadows to get closer to Tom, only about twenty yards apart. Suddenly pistol fire from Johnny found Phil's tree, and bark chips began flying off the trunk. Phil reached around the tree trunk and returned a few warning shots of his own. Johnny tossed a patio table on its side and squatted behind it. Suddenly, the three found themselves in a triangular deadlock, each about twenty yards away from the other two. Phil and Tom were happy to sit and wait for help to arrive. Johnny knew that each inactive minute diminished his window of opportunity.

"Vincent, this little game of hide and seek is over. How many more people have to die to protect you?" He looked in the direction of Phil. "You, over there. None of this concerns you. Just walk away. I'll take Vincent with me and we'll be gone."

"Can't do that. He's my responsibility. The police are on the way. You're done. Just drop your gun and give it up."

"Not gonna to happen," Johnny said. "Vincent and I have unfinished business." Then he turned back to Tom. "Vincent, you caused me a lot of trouble, and I spent a lot of money tracking you down," Johnny said.

"Good," Tom said. "Put it on my tab."

Johnny looked around and spotted a row of landscape stones at the edge of the patio, each about the size of a softball, that might offer a diversion. He leaned over to pick one up when Tom reached around his tree fortress and fired his pistol, barely missing Johnny's hand, but kicking up rocks at his feet. Johnny pulled his hand back, furious at himself for underestimating his prey.

"Vincent, I'm going to carve you up and stuff you in a fifty-gallon drum of acid," Johnny called out.

"Come and get me," Tom answered back.

Johnny bent down again and grabbed the stone, then heaved it into the brush twenty yards to the right of Tom's location, causing Tom to shift position and expose himself. Johnny snapped off a shot from his Glock and saw Tom grab his head and reel backward into the underbrush. Phil saw Tom fall and felt sick that he failed to protect Tom from these ruthless assassins. He furiously emptied his M18 in Johnny's direction, hitting the overturned table several times, but missing Johnny completely. He continued to pull the trigger a few times, but knew the clip was spent.

Johnny stood up, now confident his adversary was helpless, and fired five rounds into the tree shielding Phil, stepping forward as he fired, until he stood only fifteen feet away. Phil knew he was a dead man. He dropped his empty weapon and stepped away from the tree. He glanced over Johnny's shoulder and saw blessed reinforcements quietly approaching. For a moment Johnny felt a surge of victory that this long and arduous search for his father's obsession was finally over. I just need to tie up one loose end, he thought – eliminate the only witness that could testify against him. He turned his gun on Phil.

"Nothing personal," Johnny said, as he raised his pistol and took aim. Suddenly, a shot rang out from behind and a bullet, straight and true, sank deep into Johnny's back, dropping him to the ground. As Johnny fell, Phil could see clearly the silhouette of Sgt. Mike Belvedere, backlit in the near distance, his service pistol raised, barrel still smoking from the shot that settled this fracas.

"Took you long enough to get here," Phil said. Policemen poured into the patio to secure the area. One officer began taping off the entire patio to cordon off the crime scene. Phil made his way over to the broken body of Joe Henjum, still crumpled on the patio. He cradled Joe in his arms. Slowly Joe opened his eyes.

"You did good, soldier," Joe said softly.

"No – it was all you. You saved us," Phil said. Joe closed his eyes. Breathing seemed to take more energy than he possessed. Once more he forced his eyes open. "At least this damn cancer didn't take me," he whispered, then shut his eyes for good.

The parking lot soon clogged with ambulances and police cars. Blue, red, and white lights lit up the night, flashing in a chaotic syncopation. Even the fire engine from Billings Fire Station One muscled its way in, just in case. The fire chief hopped out of the cab and shouted orders to move cars and make way.

The hungry media, starved for sensation, routinely monitored police scanners and picked up the reports of a shooting at The Sanctuary, and dispatched reporters. In no time at all, the local radio station broadcast a special report.

"We interrupt our program to inform our listeners that a mass shooting has just occurred at a local retirement community. Police are just now arriving to take charge of the crime scene at The Sanctuary, a large senior residential complex, where it is believed five people have been killed. The names have not been released, but our reporters are on the scene, and we will update you as soon as we have further information. We now return you to our regularly scheduled programming."

In all, the police counted five bodies, including Marco, who bled out when Phil's chance hit tore his femoral artery. Tom's body was quickly bagged and whisked off to the county morgue, while the others were delivered to the Medical Center for identification and autopsy. Families, employees, and residents flooded the scene, asking questions, tingling with excitement, and sharing with anyone who would listen just how close these villains came to escaping after fulfilling their heinous intent. No one doubted that Billings had not seen such a tumult since Butch Cassidy and his gang blew through town over a hundred years ago.

The local TV channels led their 11:00 p.m. broadcast with the shootout, and the morning press gave the story front page coverage. When the story made the national news the next day, Phil knew his career was over and the facility would never recover.

Joe Henjum's body received a hero's funeral. He was laid to rest at the Yellowstone National Cemetery in Laurel, Montana, joining fellow military heroes from years past. Phil offered parting words on behalf of this decorated Marine, who touched him in the few short months they shared together.

"He was a man of courage, elegance, refinement, dignity, and virtue," Phil said. "He is now resting with his brothers."

The funeral for Tom Reese required some creative work on the part of the morticians. The public was told that the bullet struck him in the head and shattered his entire facial bone structure, which demanded considerable reconstruction to make him presentable for viewing. The embalmer used so much wax to approximate the shape and lines of Tom's face that he almost looked like a department store mannequin in his open coffin. A framed photo of Tom sat on top of the open casket for reference.

At the modest service, attendees included two gentlemen from New York. One was an elderly man by the name of Franco Giovani, Santino's brother. The other was a fit and brooding dark-haired bodyguard. Franco grew up in Sicily and immigrated to the United States at the end of World War II. He learned English growing up and spoke it with no trouble, but for the moment he chose to speak to his associate in Italian to avoid prying ears from eavesdropping. During the viewing, he took a personal interest in examining the body closely. He insisted on watching the casket placed slowly into the ground and buried. Satisfied, Franco and his associate returned to New York the next day.

Once they left, Dan Haley, with the U.S. Marshal service, asked Phil to meet him late the following night at his hotel to say good bye.

"I doubt our paths will cross again," Dan said. "So I wanted to close the book on Tom Reese, or Vincent Wallace, with full disclosure, because Tom feels you deserve it."

"Feels? You mean 'felt,' don't you?" Phil said.

"No. I mean feels," Dan said. And with that he opened the door to the adjoining hotel room and in walked Tom Reese, alive and well. Phil's mouth dropped open.

"You're not dead?" Phil said.

"No, not yet at least," Tom said.

"But I saw Johnny shoot you."

"Naw, he's not that good a shot. It was all just an act," Tom said.

"We ultimately realized that the only way Tom would ever get his life back would be when the Giovani family believes he is in fact dead. So, we took this extraordinary opportunity to fake his death and even orchestrate an open casket viewing so that any members of the Giovani family who might want to verify Tom's demise would be able to actually see his dead body."

"OK. So, who was that in the casket?" Phil said.

"We had to borrow an actual mannequin from the local department store and attach a wax figure of Tom's head for the viewing. I thought it looked pretty convincing myself," Dan said.

"Fooled me," Phil said. "So, now what?"

"Tom will disappear. Maybe move to Guam, like we discussed, or maybe Tahiti, or even Houston," Dan said.

"Houston?" Phil said.

"Sometimes there is no better place to get lost than in a crowd," Tom said. Phil reached out to shake Tom's hand.

"I got to admire you," Phil said. "You risked your life to testify against a mob boss. I don't know if I could do that. You got my respect. I'll be sad to see you go. I hate to lose residents for any reason, especially residents who pay their rent as promptly as the U.S. Marshal service does. But on the other hand, I'll be glad to see you go. I'm not sure this facility will survive the trauma we all collectively just put it through. In any case, Tom, I wish you good luck."

After reading about the death of Tom Reese/Vincent Wallace, Mr. Diamond called the secretary into his office.

"Eunice, I need you to expunge all files related to the Tom Reese case. Shred all print files and permanently erase all digital files before the day is over."

"Do you want to save any information from this file in the cloud?" Eunice asked.

"Not a single word. We run a skip tracing business finding people who don't want to be found. It would not do to have any of our subjects turn up dead due to our investigative prowess. We must never give some enterprising lawyer any reason to suspect that we participate in any conspiracy to commit murder, now do we?"

"Leave it to me. By the end of the day it will be like Tom Reese never existed," Eunice said.

# CHAPTER 37

Phil dared not show his face in the facility for an entire week. Guilt hounded him every waking minute. He hunkered down in his manager's apartment, waiting for the hammer to drop – wrongful death lawsuits, malfeasance, dereliction, and who knows what else. He knew better than to allow Tom Reese to remain, he chastised Walter for permitting it, demanded the U.S. Marshal rectify it, but still tolerated a situation that clearly put his residents in harm's way. He could blame no one but himself for Joe Henjum's death. Even though Joe's days were numbered with cancer, the moment of his last breath should have been up to God, not him. He expected a phone call any day from the home office demanding his resignation and suggesting that he retain a bulldog defense attorney. After dinner, Phil heard a knock at the door.

"Who is it?"

"Lloyd Woodward." Lloyd was the president of the resident council and always impressed Phil as a level-headed guiding force in the facility. Phil opened the door.

"Come on in," Phil said. They got comfortable in the living room. Lloyd broke the silence.

"I've called a general meeting tomorrow morning at 10:00 a.m. in the auditorium. All the residents and families were invited. I even notified your home office that we were having this meeting, and they said they would send someone down to observe. I think you really need to be there."

"I'd rather not walk into an ambush," Phil said. "Can you give me a preview?"

"A lot of residents are uncertain about the future. There's a lot of anxiety, as you might guess, so we wanted to give everyone a chance to speak their mind. You need to hear what they have to say, so you can be fully informed."

"What are you going to say, if you don't mind me asking?"

"I'd rather just wait until tomorrow. I'll say my piece in front of you and everyone."

"Fair enough. Ten o'clock tomorrow. Should I bring a flack jacket?"

"Stop worrying – the resident council can't fire you."

"Maybe not, but they can make a fella feel pretty unwelcome." Lloyd rose to leave. They shook hands.

"Get some sleep. We'll see you in the morning." After Lloyd left, Phil laid out his suitcase and packed his clothes to prepare for an inglorious departure from Billings to who knows where.

The next morning the parking lot filled to overflowing. Phil looked out his window as the line of cars spilled out into the street. A black Lincoln Town Car pulled into the parking lot. "That must be the Chicago brass," he thought. "Time to face the music." He decided to wear his "Montana" outfit, just in case it possessed magical powers to evoke sympathy from the locals.

Phil took the elevator down to the ground floor and passed through the lobby on his way to the auditorium. It was unusually empty for this time of day. "Everybody's either in the auditorium or moved out," he surmised. Then his eyes focused on what could only be a mirage or a hallucination of some sort. Sitting in the lobby framed in a glow of light was Annie Belmont. As soon as their eyes met, she grinned, stood up and walked towards him. His heart began pounding, and he suddenly felt as if he were floating off the ground.

"Annie," Phil said. "What the hell are you doing here?"

"I flew all the way back from LA last night to be at this meeting. Lloyd called me and asked if I'd come help."

"How long can you stay?" Phil asked. Annie could no longer contain herself. She smiled.

"That's the good news – the best possible news."

"What?"

"Well, I got the part."

"Is that the good news?"

"Yeah, but not the very best news of all. So, listen to this – at first the network was going to set the series in Wyoming, but the Montana Film Office offered the network a sweeter deal with all kinds of tax incentives. So, guess what – the network has decided to change the series setting from Wyoming to Montana."

"What? Really?"

"The entire show is going to be shot right outside of Billings. I'm back here for good! I get to have my cake and eat it too." Phil wrapped Annie in his arms and spun her around.

"That's unbelievable. You have no idea how much I've missed you – especially now that I'm marching into the lions' den."

"Yeah, Lloyd told me about this meeting," Annie said. "It's going to be intense. We better get inside." They walked arm in arm towards the auditorium. Phil noticed that spectators spilled out from the door into the hallway. The two wedged themselves through the crowd. Once inside the room, Phil took in the size of the audience. The room fell silent.

"What's everybody doing here?" Phil called out. "Did *The Golden Girls* get preempted, or something?" The room broke into laughter. Lloyd Woodward, the president of the resident council, spoke up from the platform.

"Mr. Branson, please join us on stage," Lloyd said. Every seat was full, and dozens stood along the side and back walls. Phil worked his way through the crowd and stepped up to the stage, where an empty seat awaited him. "That's right, just have a seat," Lloyd said, pointing to the vacant chair. Phil sat down and scanned the congregation. He saw Leland Thompson, the Chairman of United Senior Living, seated on the front row, along with three executive VPs. Phil gave Leland a polite nod. He also spotted Sgt. Mike Belvedere and Louie Gomer sitting side-by-side. Near the back, he saw Dale and Sarah Ramsey, and Darlene Longwood.

"We are ready to begin," Lloyd spoke into the microphone. "The unfortunate events of a week ago have left many wondering the kind of leadership that would permit our fine community to erupt in violence. I have been asked by many of you here what we should say to those in the media who ask if we feel safe anymore. While I cannot speak for all of you, I will share my thoughts, and then Annie Belmont, who is holding our roving microphone, and will get to you in turn to share yours." Lloyd paused and took a small drink of water from the glass on the podium. He continued.

"Three assassins from a New York organized crime family invaded our home here to kill one of our own residents and to execute anyone who might get in the way. These were determined, experienced killers who had a score to settle. Now, many of you might think Mr. Branson was no match for these cut-throats, and you'd be right. Nevertheless, he lured them away from the facility and out of harm's way, and with the help of Sergeant Belvedere, dispatched all three of them – think about that. In my book, if that is the extent to which our manager will go to keep one resident safe, then I want him here to watch over all of us." The room erupted in a standing ovation. Phil could not believe his eyes and ears. He even noticed Leland Thompson join in the applause. Lloyd quieted down the room.

"Now, I know some of you have your own opinions about Mr. Branson you'd like to share, and we want to hear them all. So, just raise your hand and we'll get a roving microphone over to you." Mrs. Walsh stood and raised her hand. Annie worked her way over and gave the mic to her.

"My name is Mildred Walsh. I've lived here going on five years now, and I just want to say that there are different ways to save a person. Several months ago I slipped and fell in my bathroom, and I was stuck there for half a day. Mr. Branson found me in time, or I might have died. So, you can think what you like, but if he goes, I go. Oh, and another thing – he made sure I got six shrimp in my shrimp cocktail." The crowd offered another round of applause.

Louie Gomer raised his hand, and Annie stepped over with the microphone. "Many of you may not know me. My mother lives here. Her name is Edith Gomer. I just want to say that Mr. Branson saved my mother from depression by giving her a reason to live. Some of you folks that moved in here the last few months know her as the Move-In Coordinator. That was a job Phil created just for her. It gave her purpose at a time when she felt worthless. And, yeah, that saved her life." Another round of applause. Mike Belvedere raised his hand for the microphone.

"I'm Mike Belvedere. I work for the Billings Police Department. My mother lives here – Irene Belvedere. Probably none of you know that only because of the integrity of Phil Branson were we able to solve the murders of two previous employees of this facility and bring their killers to justice. And he did this at great personal and professional risk. As far as I'm concerned, you're lucky to have him here."

Additional residents shared their comments for another thirty minutes. Some praised Phil for joining in the activities of the residents and making them more welcome, others for improving the food service, taking the time to listen to resident concerns, and maintaining high employee morale. Lloyd finally brought the testimonials to a close. He turned everyone's attention to the executives from the company that owned and operated The Sanctuary.

"We have the CEO of United Senior Living here today, Mr. Leland Thompson. I asked him to come and listen in to your feelings before they made a decision on the matter of Phil Branson." He turned to Mr. Thompson. "Well, sir, what are your plans for Mr. Branson?" Annie brought over the roving mic and Mr. Thompson stood up.

"I've always had a special place in my heart for this facility," Leland said. "My father grew up working on a ranch in Nebraska, and he passed on his affection for the open range to me and my brothers. I remember as a kid, he would tell us about riding his horse to the crest of a hill, where he loved to look as far as the eye can see nothing but nature untouched by humans. I got busy in the business world and never shared that moment with him. But I look around this room and I see the spirit of my father running through your veins. You could have moved anywhere to retire, but you chose Montana. Why? Because you've seen what he saw, and you feel the same way. When I sent Phil Branson out here, I sent our best man, maybe not tall in the saddle, but devoted to taking care of you as if you were my father. Everything I've heard today tells me he was the right man for the job. I recently offered him a very lucrative position with our company back in Chicago, but he turned it down, because he would rather be here with you. So, he is yours for as long as you want him." The audience rose to their feet and applauded.

"And one more thing," Leland continued. "We haven't even sprung this on Phil yet, so we're going to tell him and you all at the very same time. We are making Phil a part owner of this facility. So, from now on, when you got something to say to Mr. Branson, you won't be talking to an employee – you'll be talking to the owner." Leland looked over at Phil and gave him a nod, as the crowd registered their approval with thunderous applause.

Leland handed the microphone back to Annie. Phil waved her over to the edge of the stage.

"Did you know about all this?" he said. She grinned.

"Yeah," she said. He just shook his head. Lloyd called Phil over to the podium.

"Well, it looks like you're stuck with us, Phil. What have you got to say?" Phil stepped to the podium and turned to the audience.

"I'm very touched and just a little overwhelmed at your kind words. I knew without your support, I was a goner. But we still got a battle to regain the trust of the City of Billings after all that's happened here. And that won't be easy." Lloyd reached over and touched Phil's elbow.

"Maybe you need to see what's going on in the lobby," he said into the mic. "What do you think, folks?" A round of applause told Phil there was something he needed to see.

"C'mon, Phil. Let's go for a walk," Lloyd said. He led Phil off the stage, and with Annie by his side, Phil left the auditorium and looked down the hallway to the lobby, which was now populated with a line of families waiting their turn to speak with the marketing office.

"What's all this?" Phil asked Annie.

"They want to move in," Annie said. "We told them the office wasn't going to be open until 10:00." One son who brought his mother to get on the waiting list got out of line briefly to speak to Phil.

"I wouldn't trust my mom to anyone else. God bless you, Mr. Branson." Annie walked Phil down the line, as more prospects introduced themselves.

"They ran out of apartments a couple days ago," Annie said. "Everyone here is just signing up to get on the waiting list. You're 100 percent full."

"I'm not believing this," Phil said.

Annie slipped her fingers into Phil's hand and pulled him close.

"It looks like you're not going anywhere," she said. Phil grinned.

"I could say the same for you."

"I just have one question," she said, as she wrapped her arms around him and pulled him in close. "Where do I sign up?"

He smiled and lifted her off the ground. They kissed, not a good-bye kiss, but a welcome home kiss, deep and long, right there in the lobby, in front of residents, families, employees, God, and everyone.

THE END

Made in the USA
Middletown, DE
10 February 2021